HARD RIDE

POWERTOOLS: HOT RIDES, BOOK #3

JAYNE RYLON

HAPPY ENDINGS PUBLISHING

V2

eBook ISBN: 978-1-947093-05-8

Print ISBN: 978-1-947093-06-5

ABOUT THE BOOK

There's a thin line between love and hate.

Kyra Kado hates Van Hernandez. Or at least she wishes she could. Ever since she kissed him and he rejected her as a "mistake", things have been tense onboard their tour bus. Kyra takes out her aggression during her drumming performances as a member of Kason Cox's band and tries not to think about how well Van guards her body between their shows.

Until she meets Ollie Dawes, who's the perfect distraction. Funny, flirty, and cute AF, he takes her mind off Van. The Hot Rides salvage man is used to being alone on his solo part-finding missions, but she suspects he'd rather not be lonely anymore. She can relate. So she invites him to come see a show.

When Van discovers Kyra and Ollie performing an illicit encore together, he goes berserk. Distancing herself from Van might keep Kyra's heart safe, but what about her body? A string of unsettling incidents make Kyra afraid one of her admirers has crossed the line from fan to fanatic.

With Ollie and Van teamed up to protect Kyra, she isn't sure she'll survive being torn between the two men she craves. She might have to sacrifice her friendships with them to stay sane, unless she can think of a way to keep them both in her life or in her bed.

This is a standalone book in the Hot Rides series and includes an HEA with no cheating. The series is part of the greater universe where both the Powertools and Hot Rods books are also set, so you can visit with many of your previous favorite characters and see what they're up to now!

ADDITIONAL INFORMATION

Sign up for the Naughty News for contests, release updates, news, appearance information, sneak peek excerpts, reading-themed apparel deals, and more. www. jaynerylon.com/newsletter

Shop for autographed books, reading-themed apparel, goodies, and more www.jaynerylon.com/shop

A complete list of Jayne's books can be found at www. jaynerylon.com/books

1

Kyra laughed as she danced in a circle, wiggling her ass and pumping her fist. "Can you believe that happened? I'm so fucking happy for them."

Beside her, Ollie grinned, showing off his bright white, if slightly crooked teeth. She loved his smile. It was so much like the rest of him—full of personality, inspiring joy.

Her friend and boss, Kason Cox, had just professed his undying love for Ollie's two friends, Wren and Jordan, in front of tens of thousands of fans who'd attended their concert. He'd been nervous as fuck to publicly debut the love song he'd written for his lovers. The energy that had radiated from the mostly supportive crowd had blown him, and Kyra, away. It had been the most important performance of her drumming career and she wasn't ashamed to admit they'd nailed it.

"It was awesome. They deserve this." Ollie sighed, then joked, "I guess this makes us like friends-in-laws or something now."

"Yeah, it does." Kyra grinned and fist bumped him. Seeing more of Ollie would be fine by her. She'd gotten used to his quirky sense of humor and his quiet loyalty and, sure, the way he flirted with her every chance he got. Plus his pet hedgehog, Mr. Prickles, was seriously adorable.

From the instant she'd met Ollie at a party thrown by their mutual friends, he'd made her feel welcome and...*wanted*.

Which was something Kyra hadn't experienced in long enough that she'd nearly forgotten how it could make her heart race and her whole day brighten.

True, crowds roared every night she spent on tour. But they were pretty much in love with Kason, who was the front man and the artist behind most of their music. Hell, half the people who bought a ticket to see her play probably didn't even know her name. The way Ollie made her feel was more personal than a stranger's adoration could ever be.

She cleared her throat. In the wake of the profound sincerity Kason had displayed on stage, she realized she owed Ollie at least a glimpse of her gratitude. "You know, meeting you guys at Hot Rides has changed our lives for the better. Not only Kason's, but mine too."

"How so?" Ollie leaned his shoulders up against the exterior wall of the stadium and propped one foot flat on the cinder blocks. Was he really that casual or simply pretending as hard as she was?

"Being around you guys and the shop has reminded me of the rest of my dreams outside of being a fulltime musician. You know, the ones about friends and family and forevers. The really important stuff in life. So, thank you for that." She stood beside him so she didn't have to look directly into his eyes as she bared her soul. Kyra was only so brave, after all.

When Ollie reached across the gap between them and held her hand, she squeaked.

The connection and the warmth flowing through it gave her the courage to continue. Talking to him was easy, especially compared to Van, the last guy she'd had feelings for. He made sharing nearly impossible with his stony demeanor and cool indifference. Ollie was so different, and so approachable—she owed it to him to stop hiding her emotions, as she'd gotten used to doing around Van, Kason, and the rest of the guys in the band.

"I'm serious. It means a lot to me. *You* mean a lot to me. We haven't known each other that long, but I already consider you a great friend. So I hope it's okay if I say, I see how you keep yourself apart from the rest of the Hot Rides sometimes and their extended family. You shouldn't. You deserve those things too."

"I didn't know you were a romantic at heart." Ollie said, giving her an oddly intense look out of the corner of his eye.

She filled her lungs with cool night air, thankful for the chill that helped her stop sweating her ass off. It was both one of the hazards and perks of her job. She burned enough calories during each performance that if she wanted, and she usually did, she could splurge on an enormous ice cream sundae at each after-party without ever putting on a pound.

But sometimes, like now, it was hella inconvenient. Because Ollie kept edging closer and closer.

Kyra prayed she didn't stink.

"Want to know a secret?" he murmured as he leaned in, his shoulder-length wavy hair spilling over his shoulders as he braced a palm on the cinderblock building behind her and encroached on her personal space.

Not that she minded.

Kyra nodded. "Uh huh."

"I am too." And there it was. That flash of promise between them. No matter how many times they'd ignored it before, tonight—with love in the air and adrenaline running high after the show—there wasn't going to be any shutting their chemistry down.

She lifted her face toward his.

Ollie didn't disappoint. Unlike *some* people—ahem, Van, whom she was definitely not thinking about right then—Ollie didn't tease. He brushed his lips against hers while staring straight into her eyes. When she didn't object, he deepened their contact, sipping from her mouth with delicate, playful nibbles she absolutely would have expected from him.

Happiness and freedom rose like sparkling champagne bubbles within her. It had been so long since she'd felt like this. It brightened her like a ray of sunlight erasing a shadow from the corner of a garden. The sensation was pleasant, if not riveting. Yet.

Kyra speared her fingers into Ollie's hair, loving the way the thick waves filled her hands. She deepened the kiss, boosting that single shaft of sunshine into the equivalent of a blazing summer noon within her.

After a few more seconds spent soaking in the bliss he was imparting, she grabbed his shoulders and turned so she sandwiched him between her and the wall. If he wanted to get away, he could easily shove her aside. Again, unlike Van, Ollie didn't.

Nor did he wrench his lips from hers to declare the exchange a *mistake*.

So she leaned into him, intensifying their exchange again.

Ollie surprised her, clenching her hips in a sturdy grip and guiding them closer to his body until she was practically riding the thigh of his bent leg. His fingers hooked into the belt loops of her jeans and clasped her tight against him. Tight enough that his hard cock made quite the impression on her mound.

Now *that's* what she was talking about.

Kyra's mouth widened against his as she grinned despite their kisses. Ollie was fun, an awesome friend, and if he could feed off her energy to kiss her like this...who knew what else he was capable of?

She couldn't wait to find out.

Ollie groaned and drew her tongue into his mouth, sucking on it. Involuntarily, they began to gyrate against each other to the rhythm of their making out. Kyra could feel the beat reverberating through her even more strongly than her bass during the heaviest of the songs Kason had written.

Her breasts ached, so she rubbed them against Ollie's chest, making them both moan in the process. She hoped he'd parked his campervan close by. He lived in the retrofitted Sprinter while traveling for his job as Hot Rides' salvage man.

Though Van usually accompanied Kyra outside for her after-concert fresh-air cool-down, he was nowhere to be seen at the moment. She and Ollie could easily slip away and get rid of the clothes currently preventing her from climbing and riding him right there, right then.

She'd drag him off soon, after she'd sampled a couple more of his addictive kisses.

Or at least that had been her plan.

The door beside them slammed open, the metal smashing into the cinder blocks inches from their heads. *Holy shit!*

She jerked in Ollie's hold, though he flipped them again to pin her against the building, using his body to shield her as he reluctantly parted their mouths. Breathing hard, he glanced over in time to see what Kyra did.

Kason's head of security—Van Hernandez, who also happened to be Kyra's best friend and previous crush... okay, maybe simultaneous crush, sorry Ollie—burst into the parking lot. He half dragged, half dangled Kason's manager Rick from his meaty fist as if he was about to boot the guy out on his sorry ass.

Kyra wouldn't blame him. Rick was a dickhead.

Instead, Van froze, looking between her and Ollie then back again before recognition dawned in his usually warm brown eyes. Poor Rick bore the brunt of his renewed fury. Van flung the man, who stumbled away from the arena to keep from falling on his pretty face. "You heard Kason. Get the fuck out of here. You have no business with us anymore."

"We have a contract!" Rick shook his fist at Van.

"I'm sure your lawyers can discuss the details," Van snarled at the poor bastard. "You have thirty seconds to get off the property before I call the cops and let them know you're trespassing."

With that, Van spread his legs and crossed his arms, becoming an immovable human blockade that had more in common with a refrigerator than the average man.

Kyra sure as hell wouldn't fuck with him when he was wearing a scowl like that. For example, she hadn't done so when he'd leveled a similar one at her while lecturing her about how they worked together and therefore shouldn't make out ever again. Instead, she'd slunk away like Rick was doing now, as though she'd done something terrible. And she'd never had the guts to bring it up afterward.

Thinking of kissing Van while being so close to Ollie made Kyra squirm and nearly come on the spot. She ducked out from under Ollie's deceptively strong arm as if she hadn't been trying to crawl deeper into his embrace a few heartbeats earlier.

When Rick disappeared into the darkness of the night, Van turned toward them. His powers of observation were part of what made him so good at his job. There was no way he would miss her flushed cheeks, her swollen lips, or the hard-on causing an impressive bulge in Ollie's jeans.

She shot him a weak and awkward as fuck semi-smile. "Hey, Van."

"Kason finally ditched that asshole, huh?" Ollie seemed oblivious to the tension zinging between her and Van. He stepped right into its stream. It snapped back on him like a broken rubber band.

"Wish we all could avoid our problems so easily." Van glowered and stomped inside, slamming the door equally as hard as he had when he'd interrupted their make-out session.

Instantly, Kyra felt her blood boiling. And not from passion this time, either.

How the fuck dare he be pissed at her for enjoying Ollie and the way he made her feel? The way he accepted her. And the way he showed her that he intended to do something about whatever it was between them—exactly opposite of how Van had acted in a similar situation.

"Where were we?" Ollie asked, wrapping his hand around her waist. Unfortunately, that only made him close enough to catch her elbow with his sternum when she flailed toward the door and the man who'd vanished behind it.

"I can't go back to making out after he killed the mood like that!" Kyra's rage ratcheted up a notch that Van had stolen even that from her. She lunged for the door handle.

"Kyra, hang on. Give yourself a second to calm down before you go in there. You're going to..." She imagined he finished with *regret it*, but she couldn't say for sure because she'd already ignored his advice.

Ollie squeezed ahead of her and tried again. "Let me talk to him. I'll smooth things over. Tell him I made the first move. I didn't realize there was something between the two of you."

"There isn't." Kyra threw her head back and sucked in a few deep breaths. They did nothing to settle her and only fueled the pressure building within her. "Not going to lie, I wished there could be. But he shut that down. So he doesn't get to disapprove of me making out with any damn person I feel like kissing—or fucking, for that matter."

"Was that where we were heading?" Ollie wondered.

"Yep. So you should be pissed at him too. Goddamned cock blocker." Kyra gritted her teeth as she marched through the roadies and fans gathered in the hopes of glimpsing Kason.

Instead of foaming at the mouth, Ollie turned apologetic, making Kyra hesitate. "Look, I shouldn't have started something tonight without talking about it first. I

8

didn't mean to make things more difficult for you and for him. I consider both of you friends. Let me fix this, please."

"*Friends*?" Was Ollie changing his mind, too? Had tonight been just another *mistake*? Maybe he hadn't wanted anything other than a few stolen kisses. Kyra staggered, giving Ollie a chance to get ahead of her. She followed a few paces behind as he approached Van, who'd stationed himself near Kason once more.

Her stomach churned. Had she read the situation wrong?

Kason looked at the head of his security team and frowned. "Everything okay? He didn't give you any trouble, did he?"

"Who, Rick? No." Van gestured at a couple of the Hot Rods—Sabra and Holden—who'd been huddled up, talking with Kason. "But Ollie, that weaselly little shit that works with you? You can take him right back to Middletown. If he doesn't get out of my face soon..."

Kyra stared, her jaw dropping open. Van never pulled shit like this. How dare he act like some jealous and possessive lover when he'd flatly rejected her?

Ollie caught up to Van, breathing hard, and said, "Van, I'm sorry. I know you have a thing for her."

What? That was news to Kyra. Ollie didn't have all the facts. Didn't know how Van had turned her away. Surely Van was about to set the record straight, which would only add to her humiliation with all their friends and co-workers gathered around.

Except he didn't tell them how he'd spurned her attention. Nope.

"Then why'd you have your tongue stuffed hallway down her throat? I thought we were friends, asshole." The entire world went into slow motion then. As Kyra tried to make sense of what Van was saying and his displaced indignation, he pulled back and sucker punched Ollie.

Then everything sped up again and happened in a rush.

Kaelyn and Nola, who were married to two mechanics, Kaige and Bryce, at Hot Rods—the classic car sister shop to Hot Rides motorcycle restorations—swooped in. They protected Ollie from Van's ire. Their husbands grabbed Van, trying to force him to settle down.

Kyra exploded.

She'd never been spurred to violence against another human being before, but Van brought things out of her, dark and wild and—apparently—potentially aggressive things.

She strode up to him and kneed him square in the nuts.

Kyra shouted over the din of celebrating fans and friends who hadn't yet caught on to their altercation. "How dare you act like you want me now that someone else is interested? How many times have I thrown myself at you?"

Her voice shredded. She swore to God that if Van made her cry here in front of everyone they knew and admired, she would knee him again, twice as hard.

He grunted and looked up at her like he might try to argue if only he could force words out around the discomfort she'd put him in.

"You idiot! You didn't have the right to say jack shit to me or ruin my night. Fuck you." When he didn't apologize, she sprang at Van again. This time the women surrounding her deflected her.

"Hey, come on." Wren wedged herself between Van

and Kyra. She held out her hand. "You're going to be pissed at yourself for this tomorrow. Come with us. We'll eat a ton of that ice cream I saw in your dressing room and figure out how to handle this better."

Devra, another of their friends from Middletown, spoke to Kyra like she was a wild animal caught in a trap of her own making. She came in close and murmured so Kyra had to relax to even hear her. "Don't give them the satisfaction of seeing you upset. Let's go. You can settle this once you're thinking straight."

Kyra nodded, her body going numb. The exertion and endorphins from the show, the rush of kissing Ollie, the guilt of being caught, and the rage Van's confusing reactions had elicited had left her empty. Dazed. Traumatized, even.

Yeah, she needed a big ass sundae.

Ollie shouted her name. She jerked, but refused to look him or Van in the eye.

Devra and Wren steered Kyra toward her dressing room, bolstering her with well-meaning lies about how men were dumb while promising everything would be okay once the dust settled.

Ollie tried again to pierce the wall of people keeping them safely separated. Van shouted her name too.

"Stop. Both of you. I just want to be alone," Kyra said loud enough to be heard, though still without looking back. If everyone around her knew she was lying out her ass, they didn't call her on it.

Instead, Devra and Wren ushered her into her dressing room, then shut the door behind them.

2

Kyra's ire bled out of her in a gush that left her wobbly. She staggered to the couch and plopped onto it, burying her face in her hands.

Of course the women she'd become friends with lately didn't listen to her proclamation about craving solitude. They barged in and swarmed her, surrounding her with hugs and reassurances. Mustang Sally, the last one through the door, locked it behind her. They left the horde of their guys on the other side to deal with their own mess.

Wren took her hand and squeezed it. "I'm sorry Van and Ollie are being such idiots."

"Where do you keep the spoons?" Devra asked as she rummaged through the supplies near the fridge-freezer, pulling out the half-gallon of her favorite ice cream someone on the crew had stashed there as they did prior to each performance.

Kyra pointed and Devra took out all of the silverware. She jabbed spoons into the ice cream until it looked like it had an unfortunate run in with a porcupine or maybe Ollie's hedgehog. Damn it, Kyra didn't want to think about Mr. Prickles or his equally adorable owner right then.

Devra handed the cold brick to Kyra, who didn't hesitate. She dug in, motioning with her spoon for her friends to join her. They descended on the dessert like a pack of wolves instead of a mismatched group of unlikely allies who knew a thing or two about boy trouble.

For a few bites, they let her simply eat. As the ice cream melted in her mouth and cooled her from the inside out, Kyra realized something was missing. "Whipped cream. We need the whipped cream. Stat."

"Hell yes, we do." Sabra lunged for the fridge and withdrew a giant can. She opened the seal and popped the cap off, tipping her head back and spraying some directly into her mouth. After swallowing, she grinned. "Had to test it out for you."

"Thanks." Kyra accepted the can from her, then did the same before passing it to Nola, who was by her side. "I feel better. A little."

"Not as good as when you were making out with Ollie, I bet." Sally smirked and gestured with her spoon. "Not that I'm blaming you, by the way. He's a cutie, for sure."

"He is." Kyra smiled softly at the thought of his quiet confidence and his laidback nature, which made it so easy to talk to him. "I wish I could ignore everything else and leave with him right now. But that's too simple to be the right answer, isn't it?"

"Probably. So what are you going to do?" Wren crouched in front of Kyra and squeezed her knee. The other woman was no stranger to difficult or complicated situations. She'd managed to overcome enormous obstacles to have the loving polyamorous relationship she dreamed of. Kyra wished she could be more like that.

It was impossible.

"The only thing that makes sense. See, I sort of had/have a crush on Van." Kyra took another giant bite of ice cream and a shot of whipped cream before continuing.

"Not to burst your bubble, girl, but that was not top-secret material." Wren winced.

"Van told the guys that I kissed him?" Kyra nearly dropped her spoon. She sort of figured, from the way he'd reacted—as if she were a poisonous snake about to strike, which he'd retreated from as fast as possible—that he wouldn't have wanted anyone to know about their indiscretion.

"Ummmm, nope." Devra sighed. "But hearing that, things make more sense. I think Wren just means it's obvious that the two of you vibe off each other and you spend way more time together than most people in a platonic relationship. Hell, when I first met you, I thought you two were a couple, not only friends."

"Oh." Shit. No use trying to deny it since she'd already ratted herself out. "Well, yeah. I wanted that. I came on to him. Kissed him. He turned me down flat and made it very clear we shouldn't blur any professional lines. I don't blame him for valuing his job more than a quick fuck, since I'm apparently not girlfriend material."

More ice cream. Though, really, was there enough ice cream in the world to stop that from stinging?

"Fuck that," Wren practically snarled. "Whether or not he's ready to admit it, he cares for you. If he didn't, he wouldn't have gone Captain Testosterone out there a minute ago, would he?"

Kyra shrugged. "I don't know. Van is right about one

thing, though. I can't afford to screw up my career over a piece of ass, no matter how fine that ass might be. Whether that's ruining things over Van himself, or pissing him off by being with Ollie..."

"You're going to give up something that could change your life because Van has a stick up his tight—if fine—ass?" Devra shot her an incredulous glance.

"Yeah," Kyra said softly. "Because, honestly, I care about him too and have for quite a while. I don't know what I want. Until I figure that out, it's not fair to Ollie to keep fooling around with him. I kind of got the feeling he doesn't think of whatever we were about to do as a fling."

She recalled his secret about romance and winced.

"It could be smart to take a step back." Kaelyn nodded. "The truth is, you're all great people. We don't want to see any of you get hurt."

Too late. Because Kyra's chest ached and the ice cream was only doing so much to dull the pain.

After Wren, Kason, and Jordan's earlier example, the very last thing she'd wanted for herself was to spend another lonely night curled up in her bunk, sighing over pictures of friends with their significant others and families living their best life as she scrolled through social media. Unfortunately, she didn't see that changing any time soon.

She dropped her spoon into the empty carton along with the rest of them and slumped against the back of the couch. To no one in particular she said, "Do you think you could round up some of your guys or maybe another person from the security team to walk me over to the tour bus? Don't let Van do it no matter what he says. I won't go alone with him. Not right now. Not tonight."

"Of course," Devra said, then slipped out of the dressing room.

"It might not seem like it now, but things will be okay," Wren promised. "Keep an open mind and an open heart and you never know what might work itself out."

Kyra caught herself before making a snarky comment about fairytale endings and how they didn't seem to be her thing. Wren had fought hard for her own win and she should be celebrating it with her two men, not shut in with Kyra while she pouted over a few failed kisses.

A knock came at the door before Jordan poked his head in. He beamed at Wren then shot Kyra a sympathetic glance. "Are you okay?"

"I will be," she promised.

"I believe that, too." Jordan held his hand out to her. "I heard I have the honor of escorting you fine ladies back to the bus tonight. I'm ready whenever you are."

Despite his nonchalance, she realized he was perfect for the temporary job. As a currently unemployed ex-special agent, he might appreciate feeling useful. Who was she to take that from him?

Kyra stood, accepting a giant group hug that felt even better than her ice cream had tasted. Maybe she wasn't as alone as she'd thought. "Thank you all for giving a shit. Now, let's get the hell out of here."

If she couldn't have a hard fast ride with Ollie, or Van, to burn off her excess energy, she wanted to take a hot shower and fall asleep after her adrenaline crash so she could forget about the disaster the evening had turned into.

3

"Mr. Prickles, I was *so* right." Ollie doled out a sprinkle of mealworms on top of his pet hedgehog's dry kibble. Mr. Prickles lived in a cage that took up a disproportionate amount of space in Ollie's converted van. He didn't mind since the little guy was the closest thing he had to family. At least he had been until Ollie had joined the Hot Rides garage, inheriting a readymade team of friends in the process.

Still, Kyra had nailed it. He didn't always feel like he totally belonged. Maybe because he was the only one not attached in the group. Earlier that evening, he'd imagined that might change. "Kyra tastes even better than she looks. I could have spent the entire night standing out there kissing her. If only that muscle-bound asshole hadn't interrupted. Oh yeah, and punched me in the face."

Mr. Prickles grabbed a mealworm between his paws and stared at Ollie as he munched its head off.

"Don't look at me like that. I know Van is pretty cool otherwise. And I know I said I wasn't going to kiss Kyra since he obviously likes her, but I couldn't help it."

Ollie reached into his fridge and took out a can of root beer. He wrapped it in a dishtowel, then held it to his throbbing face. Even that didn't dull the memory of what had happened between him and Kyra.

So he explained to Mr. Prickles, "She's fire when she performs and then she was there talking about love and romance and her eyes were big and so green and... hopeful. I couldn't resist."

Mr. Prickles shook his coat, then went back for another morsel.

"Yeah, Van is pissed at me now. So is Kyra. Even still, it was worth it." Ollie toed off his sneakers, double checked the door locks, and put his reflective privacy screens in the windshield and side windows. Then he hopped up onto his platform bed. It was a few feet off the ground to make room for the storage bay beneath it, which he could access from the rear door of the van.

The king-sized mattress took up the entire back third of his home. It was huge for just him and didn't do much to make him feel less lonely, but it was comfortable as fuck—one luxury he'd refused to sacrifice when he'd chosen to live on the road.

The low cost associated with van life allowed him to spend time doing shit he enjoyed instead of running the rat race. Maybe if his father had traveled a similar route, the man wouldn't have keeled over of a heart attack in his penthouse office when Ollie was too young to even remember him.

His home might not be conventional, but it was his. And he could take it wherever life led him. Like the parking lot of concerts or to the Hot Rides garage or to salvage sites where he found the fascinating objects other people considered trash but he called treasure.

Restoring antiques to their former glory, bringing them back to life, gave him immense satisfaction and helped combat his anxiety about losing things—especially, people.

Maybe it was for the best that things hadn't worked out with Kyra.

It had been a while since he'd allowed himself to get attached to someone. He was already in the danger zone because of his connections to the Hot Rides and Hot Rods gangs. But those relationships had thawed something in him and made him crave more, maybe something deeper.

What had originally seemed like freedom as he traversed the country, uncovering and preserving rare finds, while seeing new-to-him sights, was starting to feel a lot like isolation. Especially after he'd spent the summer camped at Hot Rides, hanging out with Quinn, Trevon, Devra, Wren, Jordan, Kason, and all of the Hot Rods mechanics, their wives, kids, and parents.

It wasn't only the winter wind blowing him back toward the shop and the offer of a semi-permanent place to park his van.

The holidays were coming too quickly.

They were always rough for Ollie.

Without thinking, he rolled to the edge of the bed and opened the nearest drawer in his kitchenette, which ran the length of one wall from his bed to the van's sliding door. Inside, a small package was wrapped in festive—if faded—paper. It had a few worn edges here and there, and he'd had to retape the seams a couple of times over the decades since he'd been given the gift.

As he did often, he speculated about what might be inside.

Before he could cave to curiosity and peek at the one

corner where a tiny tear had formed recently, he slammed the drawer shut.

Just like he should close the door on whatever oopsy-tonguey had happened with Kyra earlier.

He hated to even consider the possibility, but she might only have done it to make Van jealous so he would finally pay attention to her.

He was an idiot.

Van might or might not have Kyra tonight. But even if he didn't, he at least wasn't relying on a hedgehog for company. He had the rest of the band, Kason, and any number of other people surrounding him. Ollie would gladly have traded a knee to the nuts for someone to talk to, or even another warm body nearby, just then.

He flopped onto his back, tapped the switch on the wall to extinguish the lights, and tried to pretend like he still enjoyed the deafening silence of the night, broken only by Mr. Pickles' ridiculously loud crunching. Ollie adjusted his position so he could perch the cold can on his face better. It still hurt like hell.

"You think I should text her?" he asked his hedgehog, who quit eating for a moment, letting his stillness ring throughout the interior of the campervan.

"Yeah, you're probably right. Goodnight, Mr. Prickles."

Unfortunately, Mr. Prickles didn't answer back.

4

Van scrubbed his hands down his jeans over and over, though his palms remained sweaty as fuck. He'd faced armed enemies intent on blowing his brains out during his stint in the Marines and had never once been as afraid of confronting someone as he was about talking to Kyra.

Mostly because she'd been right to rip him a new one in front of every last one of their friends and coworkers. He'd fucked up. Several times. First by allowing his interest in her to peek out, then by giving in to temptation and kissing her that one fateful day, and afterward by pretending it hadn't meant anything to him in order to maintain the professionalism required of their positions.

Only when he'd seen her making out with Ollie had he realized how badly he'd handled the situation. Because in that moment, it had been painfully obvious that his infatuation with Kyra went beyond bus-buddies or even fascination.

He might be obsessed.

Every night, lying within arm's reach without the right

to extend his hand and touch her had obviously driven him mad.

The rest of the band had left to celebrate Kason's new single hitting number one on the charts. When Van had realized Kyra was missing from the group and that Jordan was there to keep an eye on Kason's security in his place, he'd begged off, praying for a minute to talk to Kyra in private—a rare commodity in their situation.

He hoped she was on the bus and not out somewhere on her own. Both because he needed to clear the air and because he hated the idea of her wandering around unprotected. Whether she realized it or not, she was famous. More so every day and, therefore, exposed.

Sunglasses, a hat, and dark baggy clothes weren't going to be enough to obscure her identity in public for much longer. She rebelled against the loss of her freedom and despised taking bodyguards from his team with her. But that was the price she had to pay for their success.

Someday, when he wasn't already on precarious footing with her, he'd talk to her about that and make sure she quit dodging them, even if it was only from time to time.

Today, he had much more important, and more difficult, things to say.

Van tapped his code into the bus's keypad and entered. A sweep of the living areas left him disappointed. No Kyra.

Damn!

He headed toward the rear of the bus, wondering if she was taking advantage of the solitude to indulge in a bubble bath in Kason's bathroom, which she sometimes did, calling it her spa day.

Except the door was wide open, and no one was in there.

Shit!

He'd resigned himself to hanging out and waiting for her to return. As he entered the corridor between the six berths where he, Kyra, and the rest of the band slept, he realized a shadow crossed the curtain of hers. And it wasn't his own.

She was sleeping? Kyra despised naps. She thought they were a waste of time she could be doing any of the other things she enjoyed. And no one spent more time in their bunk than they really had to, at least not when they had the whole bus to themselves. Though they were fine for sleeping, there wasn't a lot of room in them for much anything else. He must have hurt her even more than he'd realized if she was in here, hiding from her problems.

Van drew a deep breath. He took a moment to compose the opening lines of his forgive-me speech as he shuffled from foot to foot. Then he tugged one corner of the curtain back as he quietly asked, "Hey, can we talk?"

Kyra gasped and froze, her eyes wide. She had headphones in, her laptop open, and her hand in her yoga pants. His bug-eyed stare winged from where she was obviously taking care of herself to the porn playing on her screen.

Fuck!

Van snapped the curtain closed again. He stood there, breathing hard, unsure of whether to run away or to dive back inside.

How could he possibly have managed to make things *worse*?

Van thought about Kason. What would he do if this was Wren or Jordan? How would he show them that he cared? He'd risked his entire career for the people he loved. Maybe Van needed to do the same to prove to Kyra that she was important to him.

"You're just going to stand there?" Kyra shrieked from inside.

"What else am I supposed to do?" he asked.

Kyra yanked the curtain apart then. Her laptop was closed and tucked into the pocket on the wall along with her headphones. She rolled onto her side and leveled a glare at him. "Anything but stand there and judge me. If I don't do something to relieve the pressure, I'm going to explode. Now get the fuck out of here so I can finish the job you obviously don't want to do."

"Don't tell me what I want," he snarled, his rational approach out the window. It was impossible to think when she was here, horny, and questioning his desire for her. She had no idea how deeply he longed for her. Mostly because he'd been very careful not to let it show. "You might be able to get away with shit like that with Ollie, but not me. I'm not nearly as nice as he is."

Kyra sat up so fast she nearly decapitated herself in the limited space of her berth. She jabbed her finger toward the door. "Get out."

"No." He leaned forward instead, bracing his hands on her bunk so their faces were inches apart and she had to look directly into his eyes. "I can't lose you. Whether letting go would be the right thing or not, I just can't. You're my best friend."

"So you want to be pals again, is that what you're saying?" Kyra tried to seem indifferent, but the fact that she closed her eyes to avoid meeting his stare despite their proximity made him certain he'd hurt her. Was still doing it, too.

And that had to stop right then or he'd never forgive himself.

"That would be the proper thing to do..." Van drew a deep breath, then admitted, "Except I'm tired of being responsible."

"Prove it." Kyra opened her eyes, shooting him a blatant dare from their emerald depths.

So Van did the only thing he could think of. He crawled into the bunk with her. The confined space didn't leave much room for air. That was one reason he could think of for how hard it was to fill his lungs while Kyra's luscious body rested beneath his.

He met her shocked gaze, mesmerized by her dilating pupils. Rings of neon green surrounded them. From this close, he noticed there were also yellow flecks he hadn't seen before. How many other nuances had he overlooked while deliberately trying not to scrutinize every luscious detail of her? It had been torture being so close and yet never allowing himself to fully appreciate her.

Enough. He was done with that.

If it meant he lost his job, so what? Jordan had walked from his for Wren and for Kason. Kason had risked his for Jordan and Wren. Shouldn't Van be willing to do the same for the woman he adored and had for years?

"Van?" Kyra wheezed.

"Yeah."

"You going to lay there like a sack of cement or are you on top of me for a reason?" She lay perfectly still beneath him, unyielding.

Maybe he'd read things wrong. Maybe she'd moved on and was waiting for Ollie to call.

No! He wouldn't go down without a fight.

Van wasn't great with words. So he showed her how he felt instead.

He settled fully between her thighs and aligned their pelvises. There was no way she'd be able to mistake the bulge of his cock against her mound. The contact made him groan.

Then there was no turning back. He dipped his head and slanted his mouth over hers.

She didn't try to kill him, so he hoped she was onboard.

When she moaned between his lips and put her arms around him, locking him to her, he kissed her in earnest. It probably made him an asshole, but seeing Ollie doing this to her had made his instincts roar. He'd been turned on, too. But mostly jealous that he wasn't the one making her melt.

The memory spurred him. He had to make sure she enjoyed what they were doing at least as much as she'd appeared to be getting off on locking lips with Ollie. Or touching herself. Son of a bitch, that vision was going to be burned in his brain for the rest of his life.

To increase his odds of beating the competition, Van let his hand wander from her shoulder inward. He lifted up just enough to allow his fingers to snake between them and cup her breast.

He'd always wanted to feel how soft her pale skin was there. It wasn't that he'd been trying to spy on her, but they lived together on a bus for God's sake. He'd glimpsed her stealth-changing or getting out of the shower more times than he could count. Hell, he'd locked himself in the bathroom and jerked off to those accidental peeps often enough that they were probably one of his top five things to fantasize about.

Sleeping directly across the aisle from her, and watching the shadows of her lithe form projected onto the curtain separating them, he'd swear he'd even seen her doing the same once or twice. At least he liked to imagine he had. Especially after what he'd just interrupted. It was going to become his new favorite thing to recall as he touched himself, he was sure.

Or maybe what they were about to do instead.

Because he didn't have to pretend anymore. Van kneaded her like he'd wished he could have all those nights they spent so close and yet so far apart. His hands tingled finally being filled with her instead of only the thoughts of what it might be like to touch her intimately.

Kyra moaned into his mouth and arched against him.

He was glad to accommodate her unspoken request. Van increased his grip and flicked his thumb over her pierced nipples. He'd always guessed at what it would be like to suck on them.

No wonder he'd damn near killed himself attempting to appear indifferent. Did she have any idea how difficult she'd innocently made it to concentrate on his duties by being so fucking sexy?

Around her, his professionalism was always on the verge of collapse. And now...

It was too late to salvage it.

Van groaned when Kyra wrapped her legs around his hips and began to rub against him in a full-body hug. Her core cushioned his steely cock and tempted him with the lushness he was sure he'd find beneath her cotton pants.

Kyra wrenched her mouth from his. For a moment he was terrified she was going to put the brakes on. Remind them of their careers and the millions of reasons why what they were doing was a horrible idea. Instead, she cried, "More! Van, I want more."

He couldn't deny her when he needed the same things she did.

But Kyra had obviously had enough of waiting for him to make it happen. She fisted the hem of his black tour T-shirt and dragged it over his head before flinging it to the ground between their berths. When her callused palms ran over the expanse of his back from shoulders to his ass, she reminded him of exactly how damn strong she was even if she shivered beneath him.

It was a gift, one that meant the world to him, that she let him take charge. So he embraced his instincts and prayed she liked what she saw in him when the facade of civility and professionalism crumbled.

Van curled his fingers in the waistband of her pants and the panties she wore beneath, yanking them both down. He used his knee even as she squirmed, freeing one of her legs. That was good enough. She was bared to him, even if her other ankle was still shrouded in her clothing.

He gripped her hips, then shoved her upward, some part of her—either her head or her shoulder—knocking into the wall hard enough to make a distinct *thunk*. But she didn't tell him to stop, so he didn't.

Van wormed in the opposite direction, as far as the bunk would allow. He bent his legs at the knees so he could lie on his stomach between Kyra's thighs. The scent of her arousal made his nostrils flare. His mouth watered and his tongue flicked, lapping the first taste of her from her skin.

Kyra flung out one hand, slapping it on the wall of the berth.

He chuckled against her flesh, taking that as a good

sign, then dedicated himself to blowing her mind. If he had anything to say about it, she'd never masturbate again. Not because he had some kind of problem with that, but because he was happy to give her as much pleasure as she could stand.

Van buried his face in her pussy. He traced her with the tip of his tongue, memorizing the topography of her body and mapping the spots she reacted to the most. He suckled her clit in between exploratory voyages along her cleft. When she began to moan and her ragged breaths echoed in the berth, he slid his hand across the top of her thigh and inward.

"Fuck, you're good at that," Kyra sighed, then stiffened as he added his hand to the mix. He probed with his middle finger, testing the opening of her pussy, finding it as tight and tempting as he'd always imagined it would be. When she finally let him in, the barest bit, he swore she scorched him. Still, he didn't pull away, not now that he was poised on the brink of penetrating her. Neither of them could have resisted the attraction zinging between them then.

Kyra gyrated beneath him, helping his finger drill inside her inch by inch.

She gripped his head, unable to find purchase in his ultra-short hair. Maybe he'd have to let it grow out, like Ollie's. Damn, why was he thinking of the other guy now?

Van focused on Kyra and the way her body was pulling him inside, surrounding him with liquid heat. She was so soft and slick that his cock leaked in his pants. Though he wasn't about to stop eating her long enough to give his dick what it craved, not yet, he redoubled his efforts.

His index finger joined his middle finger inside her as he teased her clit with his tongue.

"Van!" Kyra shouted, making him feel ten feet tall. For that matter, so did the berth, which limited his motion. Something about it also made it seem like they were tucked together away from the rest of the world, wrapped in a cocoon of pleasure he wasn't eager to leave anytime soon. When they did, what would their relationship have evolved into?

He couldn't think about that either.

All that mattered was infusing Kyra with as much rapture as possible. Showing her that he'd never meant to wound or offend her. This was what he'd always wanted instead.

Van ate her while his fingers fucked her, spreading apart to stretch the tight rings of muscle he couldn't wait to feel massaging his cock. He hummed as she bowed, mashing herself tighter to his mouth. Her thighs clamped around his shoulders, reminding him again exactly how powerful she was and how her performances had honed her muscles.

He looked up her body, past the sexy-as-fuck tattoos on her abdomen that shifted as she flexed and released the tension beneath them. So he saw it when she reached the point of no return.

Kyra gasped. Her whole body froze and her head tipped forward so that she was staring directly at him. "Van, I'm going to—"

She never finished her sentence because he nodded, the motion stimulating her further. He pressed his fingers deep within her, curling them upward so he could press against the place that seemed to drive her wildest.

A scream ripped from her chest as she clenched

around him, threatening to break his fingers with the force of her orgasm. Van couldn't say what made him do it, but he took his mouth from her just long enough to bite her thigh lightly before concentrating on sucking her clit as she came, shuddering beneath the onslaught of her release.

She moaned over and over as he rubbed her from the inside, drawing out her pleasure.

And when she finally grew silent and went limp, he knew it was only the beginning.

Van managed to jam his hands beneath himself and undo his fly before peeling his jeans down to the tops of his thighs, barely far enough to free his cock. He didn't bother with anything more, couldn't stand to waste a moment on unnecessary motions.

He cupped Kyra's ass and yanked her toward him, equally as turned on by the crooked smile she leveled at him as she recovered from her endorphin rush as he had been by the throes of her passion.

"You didn't think I was done, did you?" he growled against her lips as they aligned more completely, his body blanketing her much more pliant one.

"I hoped not, but..." She didn't finish her thought.

It didn't matter, he knew what she was thinking. "I've let you down so often, you didn't think I'd see this through?"

Kyra nodded.

"That changes now. Today." He took his cock in his hand and stroked it a few times, mentally promising them both he'd never deny them this again. "I'm sorry, Kyra."

She reached for him then, shoving his hands away so she could wrap her fingers around his length now that he'd given them both permission. Her touch nearly made him erupt. Though some dirty part of his mind loved the thought of her glazed with his come, he had bigger, better plans for that moment.

Van smiled wickedly down at Kyra. "If you want my cock, put it in you."

"The question has never been whether *I* want *you*." She hesitated, then muttered, "You bastard."

He stared at her in shock. "If you want to see precisely how much I've been dying for you, go ahead. Put me inside you so I can show you."

Kyra stared straight at him as she aimed his cock at her opening and tugged, drawing him closer.

The moment his dick collided with her pussy, he felt the contact throughout his entire being. Her heat and the welcome of her body made him lose his mind. He fell forward, supporting himself on his palms, which planted themselves on either side of her head so as not to crush her, then slid home.

Or at least he attempted to. It took several passes, plunging deeper on each one, before Kyra could take all of him. He didn't dare hold back or give her less than everything he had because he knew she'd see that as an insult.

So he dipped his head and took her lips as he began to move, hoping he wasn't causing her discomfort when he began to pump his cock into her.

She encouraged him by raking her hands with their short, neat nails down his back, digging in when she reached his ass. Her pussy gloved him to perfection, whiting out rational thought and leaving him to pure instinct.

So Van did as she directed. He plowed into her, shaking

the entire bunk with the momentum of his thrusts. He fucked Kyra relentlessly, with years of pent-up lust and longing. She met him stroke for stroke, the percussive slap of their bodies coming together reminding him of the rhythms she set for the band. The reverberations rang like thunder in his ears.

Or maybe that was the sound a bunk made as its bolts ripped out of a bus wall.

Because next thing he knew, they were falling. Together.

He rolled, taking the brunt of the impact as they dumped out onto the floor of the bus three feet below. Unfazed, Kyra threw her head back. She looked like a goddess as she laughed, never once faltering in her motions. She swung her hips over him, riding him to the tempo they'd set.

Seeing her like that, rising over him and taking what they'd both craved for so damn long, Van couldn't hold back. He growled her name, whether in warning or triumph, he couldn't say.

Kyra bit her lip and nodded. "I'm there too. Come with me this time, Van. Please."

It was that single tiny word that did him in.

She wasn't the sort of woman to beg for anything. And when she broke and did it, he wasn't about to make her ask twice.

Van clasped her hips and fucked up into her as deep as he could go. He thrust several times before she froze and compressed around him, screaming his name. He roared hers as his orgasm ripped through him, triggering his release.

He poured himself inside of her, flooding her with every drop of his ecstasy.

It went on for so long that when his climax ended, and they quieted, the hush rang in his ears.

Kyra flopped onto his chest, her forehead resting on his collarbone as she struggled to catch her breath. He wrapped his arms around her, holding her as close to his heart as he could. It felt so right. Nearly perfect. He never wanted to let go.

They might have had to talk about what had happened and decide how to move on from there. He wasn't sure about that part now, since he'd planned to iron out all those wrinkles before sleeping with her. Except right then a beep came from the front of the bus. It was the sound of the digital keypad being unlocked. Someone was about to come onboard.

Kyra's eyes widened. She bolted to her feet—making him pound the floor as their bodies separated too soon and too abruptly for his liking—grabbed her pants from the wreckage of her bed, then dashed for the bathroom, locking herself inside. Van was standing there, his semi-hard dick hanging out, still wet with the proof of Kyra's pleasure. He put his back to the door, trying to zip up without slicing his junk off when Kason, Jordan, and Wren entered the corridor, heading for their bedroom at the back of the bus.

Situating himself, barely in time, Van spun around so they hopefully wouldn't notice the scratches on his back, which stung despite the air-conditioning washing over them, now that the glow of his orgasm was wearing off.

"Hey Van," Kason called as the steady thump of his crutches came nearer. "What're you doing? Sleeping during the day? That's not like you."

Yeah, Van was notorious for his no-napping stance. It was many of the things he and Kyra had in common. Even on long road trips, he'd rather stare out the window than be unconscious. Sleeping felt like a waste to him. Though he definitely would have preferred to be wrapped around Kyra in a nice soft bed right then.

"Uh, no. I heard something and came to see what was going on in here." Van had no way to explain his lack of a shirt or the destruction he'd caused.

Wren's gaze lasered on his chest. He tried not to look, but when he glanced down, the clear red marks Kyra had given him with her teeth and nails stood out like a neon sign advertising what they'd been up to.

And that was before Kason realized the band's bunks were in disarray.

When he saw the mangled platform that Kyra used to sleep on littering the floor, he tipped on his crutches. Jordan put an arm around his waist to steady him.

Right about then, Kyra emerged from the bathroom. Whatever she'd done in there, it couldn't scrub away the alterations to her face, which seemed more relaxed than it had in ages. Her hair stuck out, rumpled like it was after she sweated her way through a show. Despite the precarious situation they found themselves in now, she shot Van a secret smile.

"What the fuck happened here?" Kason asked, his gaze flying between Kyra, Van, and the busted berth.

"I'm not sure, but it looks like it was a hell of a lot of fun," Wren teased as she squeezed past the guys toward Kyra. The two women had become close friends during the time they'd spent lately, both on the road and at the Hot Rides garage, where Wren was a specialty welder.

Kyra smirked and Wren high-fived her, "Atta girl."

"About damn time," Jordan muttered. Van had started hanging out with the guy more often now that he was around Kason a bunch, and they had a shared background in government service and security. Hell, maybe Van should talk to Kason about recruiting Jordan. They could use someone as skilled as him on the team.

"What you two do on your off time is your business," Kason said cautiously. "But what happens between you impacts us all around here. Are we good now?"

"So motherfucking good," Kyra sighed as she dropped her head onto Wren's shoulder. The other woman hugged her and grinned.

"What she said." Van grinned and wished it was him holding Kyra instead. But he'd take what he could get until they had a chance to really work things out once and for all.

Hopefully what they'd done would make it easier and not harder to talk.

5

Kyra had needed to get away.

She wasn't sure how to feel. Excited that she'd had the best sex of her life. Satisfied that Van had seemed floored by it too. Hopeful that this could lead to more. Guilty that she hadn't thought once about Ollie before fucking Van's brains out.

Well, that last one was really more like a sickness in her stomach. She prayed she hadn't done something that would hurt Ollie, make him believe he wasn't good enough, like Van had done to her so many times. In fact, he was again since he'd rushed to have one of their staff handymen fix her bunk before the rest of the band had returned then put on such a good show for them, that even she thought maybe she'd imagined how they'd got it on.

Except her body hadn't been able to forget it. Every time she shifted, she could feel where he'd used her so well. So how had he moved on, like it had been nothing?

Confused.

Yup. That's really what it came down to. She was so

fucking lost, she needed to find herself again. Only then would she be able to figure out what was best for her and go after it.

For some stupid reason, she'd thought maybe a long walk by herself would do the trick.

Since Van would object to her assessment, maybe even more now that he had staked some sort of claim on her with every thrust of his hips between her legs, she'd slipped out while he'd been busy verifying the IDs of local laborers who would help set up before sound check.

Lost in her thoughts, she'd meandered farther away from the tour bus than she'd intended. She paused, blinking at the gray sky that promised a coming winter storm. Thank God their show tonight was at an indoor arena.

She missed summer shows, where they played outdoor amphitheaters in the sweet evening air. Fortunately, they would be headed south again soon, making a detour for Middletown, where they'd spend their next break between legs of the tour.

Kyra hustled back toward their base in yet another unfamiliar city. Damned if she could even remember where they were. Maybe that was a sign she was getting burnt out or needed a change. Like the one Ollie had offered her before everything had gotten complicated— some time away from the band, with him, at Hot Rides.

Yeah, this walk hadn't resolved any of her issues. It had only made her cold.

So Kyra picked up the pace. She cut through an alley that snaked behind the arena, which she could see a few blocks over now.

At least she'd come to one conclusion. She needed to talk to Ollie as soon as possible, and be honest about the new development in her love life. Because if she could make something work between her and Van, she wanted that.

Her heart cramped thinking about giving up Ollie, though. She'd come to lean on him to brighten her days. He was an incredible listener. Even now, she felt shitty that she wished she could hash things out with him for her own sake. Had she ruined one good thing for another?

Or worse, killed two friendships with one fuck that Van was already regretting.

Kyra decided she'd do the next best thing. She'd reach out to Wren and Devra. Maybe they could videochat when she returned to her freshly repaired berth, assuming Van was still busy at the venue. They would know how to handle a situation like this, seeing as they were each in a relationship with two men.

It was a lot more work than Kyra had realized, juggling two potential boyfriends.

What if she could have the same thing as the Hot Rides ladies? Would she even want that kind of drama?

Before she could really consider the possibilities, a noise startled her. Some sort of rustling combined with the skittering of a stone up ahead, as if someone had tripped. Except there wasn't anyone there as far as she knew.

"Hello?" Kyra called out as she poked her head around the dumpster near the corner, half-expecting to find Van or Kason or some other band member playing a prank on her. At least, that's what she was hoping to discover. "Which one of you assholes is trying to freak me out? It's not going to work."

The clang of a slamming door made her jump.

Was it the sound of someone leaving or someone joining her in the secluded space?

Damn it, why hadn't she at least told one of the roadies where she was going? No one even knew she was out here. Stupid!

Instead of one of her friends or some delusional stranger lurking in the shadows, she saw the glint of something silver bobbing about three feet off the ground. As it brushed the brick wall of the building, it made the scuffing sound she'd heard. Not a person at all. A freaking mylar balloon. Her eyes followed the attached ribbon downward to a small bouquet of grocery store roses, which it was tied to. A card peeked out from beneath them.

Kyra checked both behind her, in front of her, and around the corner.

Still no one.

So she returned to the gift left by the trash. Had someone thrown it out? Why?

When she bent down, she saw four letters scrawled onto the envelope of the card. Her name. Son of a bitch!

Someone *had* been following her.

Or...maybe... She should stop being so damn paranoid. Van's overprotective nature was rubbing off on her. The gift could be from him.

Maybe he simply didn't know how to approach her after they'd been so intimate yet resolved exactly nothing regarding their relationship, which had all the same challenges it had before they'd given in to temptation. Plus a few more their impetuous liaison had caused.

She crouched down, plucked the card from the flowers, and tore it open. All the while, she kept her head up, staying observant, just in case. When she glanced down at the card, her hand shook bad enough that she dropped it. It fluttered to the ground in a spastic semblance of a spiral that did nothing to ease the disquiet building in her gut.

Her instincts had been right. She hadn't been alone in the alley.

And it hadn't been Van offering her a sweet olive branch.

Time to get out of there. Pronto.

With one final look around, she got to her feet, prepared to race for the bus, or the backdoor of the stadium. Calculating which was closer, she paused.

When her phone buzzed in her pocket, Kyra nearly shrieked.

She clutched her chest and whipped her head from side to side, equally relieved to see there was still no one lurking around the corner and no one there to witness her overreacting. As the only female member of the band, the very last thing she needed was for them to think she couldn't handle herself.

Kyra jammed her hand into the pocket of her romper and withdrew her phone. She patted the pocketknife next to it, too.

Her anxiety dissipated further when she tapped the screen and a picture of Mr. Prickles flashed onto it. He was nibbling on a miniature sign made out of cardboard. She figured Ollie had "helped" the hedgehog write *Ollie told me he's sorry. Please forgive him.*

Her instantaneous grin faded when she realized it was she who probably owed him an apology, or at least some truth that he wasn't liable to enjoy hearing. That was scarier than some random fan leaving her presents. She chided herself for being afraid of lovely flowers, a balloon, and a note. Even if it was from a guy who kind of creeped her out even with Van around, never mind when she thought of bumping into him in an empty alley.

However, she didn't go back to collect the gifts and neither did she dally as she headed directly for the bus. At least she could be alone there to think and have a moment to recover in peace. Okay, in solitude. Because if Van saw her now, he'd notice something was off.

The absolute last thing she wanted to do was tell him what had happened. Most likely she was jumping at her own shadow. Especially since she'd let him inside her, he was going to be even more controlling than before and she didn't want him to view her that way—as some helpless charge he was responsible for sheltering.

That's how they'd gotten in this mess in the first place.

Still, she wasn't taking any chances.

Running through her options, Kyra settled on the one that seemed the most harmless. Maybe because of Ollie's message, which reminded her there were people who cared for her outside of the band for the first time in a long time. She drew out her phone and dialed Hot Rides. Someone there would stay on the phone with her until she made it safely back to the bus even if they didn't realize they were chaperoning her.

It rang once. Twice.

Then someone picked up. *Please let it be Devra. Or Wren. Or any of the guys except...*

Ollie said, "Hot Rides, how can I help you?"

The universe hated her.

"Hello?" he asked.

Kyra debated hanging up, but a crash from the dumpster behind her made her think twice. Had her overzealous fan been hiding out in the trash? Would he be pissed that she'd spurned his gifts? She hastened her steps, nearly jogging now. "Hey, Ollie."

"Kyra?" He sounded like the air whooshed out of his lungs, similar to how she felt, though probably for different reasons. Worse, she couldn't even say she'd tried to talk to him after getting his message since she'd called the shop line instead of his personal phone.

Her guts knotted, unused to so much turmoil at once.

"Um, yeah. Hey. Hi." How was she going to explain why she didn't have the right words at the moment to beg his forgiveness for storming out on their kiss and fill him in on how things were going? When had everything gotten so damn complicated?

"Are you okay? I can hardly hear you." Ollie sounded like he was moving then, maybe closing the door between the office and the shop.

Kyra cleared her throat and tried to act like everything was fine, but it was impossible. Everything was definitely *not* fine. Not in her personal life and maybe not even on a more basic level. Though she hadn't intended to be so honest, she heard herself say, "I think so. But, I'm not entirely sure. Would you stay on the phone with me for a couple minutes?"

"Of course. What's wrong?" He seemed to go on high alert. "This isn't about my text is it? Hopefully, it didn't make Van pissed at you or something."

"No." She was quick to squash that notion. "Nothing like that."

"You sound scared."

"I am." She bit her lip to keep it from wobbling. How could he read her so damn well when everyone else, especially the one man who supposedly knew her best, seemed oblivious to her emotions sometimes? "It's probably stupid..."

"No. It's not. If your instincts are telling you something's wrong, then you should get the hell away from whatever is setting you off. Where's Van?" Ollie wondered.

"We kind of got in a fight." She rolled her eyes. "Okay, no. That's a lie. We fucked. And then we freaked out about it. So we're doing our own things and pretending like it never happened."

"Does that mean you're out on your own without security and something spooked you?" Ollie was raising his voice now. Oh God, all she needed was for the Hot Rides—and the half of Middletown they were related to or friends with—to go on high alert. She's almost rather he'd focused on her admission that she'd slept with Van. Of course, Ollie being Ollie, he put her first. "Where's Jordan? I'm sure he'd stand in for Van."

"You know, you're right. I should have asked him to. I will next time. I'm almost back at the bus. Passing the arena now and have less than a block to go. Would you... would you mind talking to me until I get there, even though I was a total bitch and haven't called you to talk about what happened or where we stand? Especially after...you know, with Van."

He should probably hang up on her. It was what she would do if she were him.

But he didn't.

"We can deal with that later." His voice was tight, whether because of what she'd told him about her and Van or because of her current situation, she wasn't sure. Probably both. "Keep moving and stay calm."

"I am. Mostly. More now that I'm talking to you." She

laughed nervously. It had been stupid to bug him, or any of the Hot Rides, just because her self-proclaimed Number One Fan had left her a present to go with the ones he'd brought her at meet and greets in the past. But really, who followed a band around the country and went to every single one of their shows just to flatter their drummer?

Some people would probably consider her a bitch since instead of appreciating his unbalanced admiration, she got kind of creeped out by it.

That had been bad enough, but now he was leaving stuff for her outside of official meet and greets or his recent trick of handing it to a security guard and asking them to pass it to her for him. Had he followed her? How else would he have known she'd stumble on his offering there?

The thought gave her goose bumps. Until Ollie interrupted her worrying with something even more dreadful.

"Kyra, I can hear your breathing. It's too fast. Too ragged. You're upset." Ollie didn't ask, he knew, and she didn't dare deny it. "Listen to me carefully. There's nothing to forgive between us. I appreciate you being up front about you and Van. I can't even say I'm shocked. I knew there was something between you two from the first time I met you both. But you've got to do one thing for me…"

"Anything." She wished he was there so she could smother him in the biggest bear hug in the history of the universe. He deserved that and so much more. He was an amazing guy. One she wished she'd met at another time and in another place, when her life was simple.

"Tell Van about whatever just happened."

"Not that." She gritted her teeth.

He chuckled. "If you don't, I will. I care more about your safety than your opinion of me. Sorry."

"Ollie." She groaned. "Why do you have to be so fucking *good* all the time?"

"Bad habit." He sighed as if she'd accused him of picking his nose or something. "And for the record, if you and Van can figure shit out, then I'll be happy for you. But if you change your mind, well, you know where to find me. The campervan door is always open for you. And... Mr. Prickles misses you. You should call more often. I hated knowing you were mad at me."

Kyra's heart cracked a little because she'd missed Ollie, too. She hadn't had the guts to face him in case he severed their friendship completely. She should have known better. "I will. I promise. I wasn't pissed at you, I was worried you wouldn't want to talk to me after how I acted last time I saw you and...since."

"We're good, Kyra. Although I wouldn't take back kissing you for anything, I appreciate more about you than how you tasted. Van, too. You've become good friends and I don't want to screw that up. Hell, for that matter, you guys should come visit. Wren told me Kason is going to be here all next week on a tour break. We could hang out. You could even come on a salvage run with me if you're still into the idea, like we talked about before."

"You really wouldn't mind? What if Van comes, too?" Kyra winced. "To Hot Rides, I mean. He usually hangs out at Kason's house with me, but I figure Wren, Jordan, and Kason might want some privacy this time."

"Other than when he planted his fist in my face, I think Van's pretty cool. And I don't blame him for hitting me."

"I do." Kyra still hadn't worked everything out with

Van, that detail included. And now that they'd fucked, it might be twice as hard to make him understand her boundaries. She bounded up the stairs to the bus, shutting the door firmly behind her and testing it. Relief washed over her. "Okay, well, I'm back inside the bus. Thank you."

"Did you lock the door?" he asked.

"It locks automatically," she told him.

"Is anyone else there?" Ollie might usually seem like a playful puppy, but this inner guard dog he revealed appealed to her whether she wanted it to or not.

"No. Only me." She toed off her shoes and headed for her bunk, trying not to think about what she and Van had done there while she was still chatting with Ollie.

"Humor me and take a look around. Make sure all the windows are shut and nothing is out of place before I go." He said it as if it was a suggestion, but she was certain that if she didn't assure him those things were true, he'd be dialing Jordan and asking him to relay the message to Van in a flash.

Sometimes having friends was a pain in the ass.

Still, Kyra did it. And to be honest, it made the last of the tension melt from her shoulders and neck. Her voice wasn't shaky anymore when she said, "Everything's good. I'm good. There was nothing to worry about."

"Okay, great." Ollie cleared his throat. "It was nice to hear your voice. Call me whenever."

"Thanks. I will." Kyra put her hand over her eyes, wondering how she was going to manage her friendship and low-key flirting with Ollie at the same time as something...more...with Van.

If that's even what Van wanted. Who knew since they hadn't discussed it?

It could be that he'd gotten what he'd been looking for and was satisfied with one afternoon of bunk-breaking sex.

"If you're sure everything's all right, I better get back to work. I was just dropping a few things off from yesterday's run before I hit an estate sale this afternoon."

"Oh yeah, of course. Sorry."

"I'm not," he echoed her earlier sentiment. "Be safe, and good luck for your show tonight."

"Thank you, really." Kyra disconnected, hoping he realized that she meant for more than his well wishes. Ollie made her feel safe in a way Van's physical protection couldn't always accomplish. Their bond meant something to her, and she was afraid of breaking it, especially when he'd made it clear he'd like to do exactly the opposite.

Had she made a giant mistake?

6

O llie didn't fuck around. That wasn't his style.
Besides, he didn't have enough friends as it
was. He couldn't afford to lose any over dumb
shit.

So a week after his call with Kyra, when he heard a
shriek and poked his head out of his campervan in time to
see Wren sprint from the Hot Rides motorcycle shop's
garage toward Kason and Jordan, who'd climbed out of a
familiar monstrous black truck, he stood up straight and
prepared to man up.

Wren flung herself at her boyfriends. Jordan had
joined Kason for the most recent portion of his tour,
seeing as he was currently unemployed and Kason had
required some assistance before getting his cast off his
recently broken leg. While they reunited in a flurry of
hugs, kisses, and laughter that ended up with all three of
them tumbling to the ground in a heap, Ollie's gaze slid
behind them.

Van, Kason's official bodyguard and head of his
security detail, climbed down from the driver's side of his

truck while Kyra hopped out of the passenger-side door. Unlike her usual bubbly self, she hung back, her gaze flicking between Van and Ollie.

Did she think they were going to fight again?

He hated that he'd had any part in making her uncomfortable or unsure.

Ollie stepped down onto the brown grass, which crunched beneath his sneakers, and marched right up to Van. He stuck out his hand. "Kyra told me things have heated up between you two. Congratulations. I hope you're both going to be really happy together."

Van blinked. He glanced at Kyra, who winced. But instead of turning to Ollie with a snarl or answering his proposed truce with another black eye, Van grabbed Ollie's elbow and half-led, half-dragged him to the periphery of the gathering of Hot Rides that poured from the garage to welcome their friends home. "She told you?"

"Yeah. Don't be pissed at her for that. There's nothing to hide..." Ollie looked over his shoulder to where Kyra was hugging Quinn and Trevon in greeting. He tried not to be jealous, but he wasn't entirely successful.

"That's not what I'm worried about. What did she say exactly? About me...or us..." Van let his cool, calm, in-control demeanor slip. Ollie thought he might have been meeting the man behind the bodyguard for the very first time. Van had never seemed vulnerable before, not to force or feelings. "Because I have no fucking idea where I stand with her."

"To me, it sounded like you were lying down—not standing." Ollie winked, although part of him shriveled inside as he acknowledged that meant he was less likely to have the same experience anytime soon.

Considering how deeply her kiss had affected him, sex

with her would likely ruin him for anyone else. Maybe it was for the best they hadn't gotten that far. He had no doubt that if Van hadn't interrupted them that night, he and Kyra would have ended up in bed.

So close, and yet...

Van barely managed to suppress the grin twisting the edges of his mouth, but his satisfaction shone through his dark eyes anyway. Ollie reminded himself that he shouldn't be envious if that's what Kyra had wanted. Fuck it, though. He was.

"Anyway," Ollie dug at the dirt with the torn toe of his sneaker. "She told me you slept together. And that now things were awkward. That's it."

"Accurate." Van scrubbed one hand over his face. "Damn it. I don't know what to do next. Do I leave her alone, like I should have considering we work together in a place where working together also means living together? Or should I show her how badly I want her and always have?"

"You're asking me?" Ollie dropped his head back. "This is torture. You know that, right?"

"Yeah. Sorry." Van scrunched his eyes. "But I know you care about Kyra, and I intend to do what's best for her. I'm not sure I can really think that clearly about it at the moment when what I want..."

"Is burning you up from the inside?" Ollie sighed. "I get that."

Unlikely allies, they stared at each other for a few moments. It figured—the only person who truly understood how Ollie felt about Kyra was the other man who felt the same way.

They were screwed.

"What are you two whispering about over there?"

Devra teased as she rounded the corner of the garage closest to them, causing Ollie and Van to spring apart guiltily.

"Stuff!" Ollie shouted, his heart pounding. How much had she overheard and would Kyra be pissed if she knew they were conspiring, even if it was to bring her joy?

The woman—who was married to both Quinn, the Hot Rides shop manager, and Trevon, one of the mechanics who worked there—drew up short at the intensity of his reaction, her intuition prodding her to dig deeper. "Is it Kyra's birthday or something?"

Van shook his head. "Not until next month."

Of course Van actually knew when her birthday was. He'd known Kyra way longer than Ollie had, and they were closer. In every possible way. It was time for him to accept that and back off before he ruined his friendship with her over something that had never been meant to be.

If only he could erase the memory of their kiss, which had felt far too right to be ignored.

Nah, he wouldn't scrub that from his brain even if he could. It had been a highlight of his existence. He needed to stop thinking about it before he got hard, though. He didn't need another dent in his skull from Van's knuckles.

"Okay, well." Devra eased past them and shot them a warning look over her shoulder. "You boys play nice, whatever it is you're up to. No more fighting."

"Promise." Van cleared his throat and returned his focus to Ollie when Devra disappeared among the gathering of their friends. "Sorry about that, by the way. I, uh, shouldn't have lost control like that."

"Shit, Van. You're human, aren't you? Is it losing control you regret or is it that you have emotions in the first place?" Ollie couldn't help but commiserate. "You're not a robot. Of course it pissed you off to see me making out with the woman you have a thing for. I'm not sorry I did it, mind you, but I am sorry seeing me kiss Kyra upset you."

Van didn't respond verbally. Instead he nodded, his jaw clenched. Ollie figured that was about as much as he could expect from the other guy, who wasn't much for heart-to-hearts under the best of circumstances. In that way, they were pretty much opposites. Ollie had learned early on that if you didn't share your feelings when you had a chance, you might never get the opportunity to do it again.

Just like with Kyra. At least he'd gotten to kiss her once.

She knew how he felt about her even if they never took it any further. So he had no regrets about that night.

They turned so that they were shoulder to shoulder, leaning against the far side of the garage, then. With the difficult topic out of the way, Ollie figured Van wouldn't mind taking a turn answering one of his questions about Kyra before they headed back to the rest of the gang. His concern for her was something they had in common.

Plus, he'd given Van what little information he had, so maybe Van would appease his curiosity. "So what was up the other day?"

"Which day?" Van shuffled guilty. "The day we broke her bunk? I mean, she told you..."

"You two seriously fucked the bed into oblivion?" Ollie snorted, imagining their faces. Then he shook his head as his mind wandered to other parts of Kyra and what she might look like while someone, maybe him—or even Van —was pleasuring her like that.

"Yeah. But if that's not what you were talking about, what did you mean exactly?" Van narrowed his eyes.

"The day last week when Kyra called me because she got scared in the alleyway walking home. I got the feeling she thought someone was following her." Ollie frowned. "She did tell you about that, right?"

Van glowered.

"Right?" Ollie repeated, though he was certain the problem wasn't that Van hadn't heard him.

"*Kyra!*" Van bellowed as he launched himself toward the open garage bays, where she'd disappeared inside with Wren, Kason, Jordan, Devra, Quinn, Trevon, and god knew who else.

There were always people around. But the past few days had been especially busy as the mechanics from their sister-shop, Hot Rods, and their families popped over a few at a time to check out the two new employees who'd come onboard a few days ago.

Ollie figured they didn't want to swarm the place all at once and overwhelm the pair of machinists, but they were too curious and protective of their "little brother" Quinn, who managed Hot Rides, to stay away for long.

Roman stuck his head out to see what the ruckus was about. Van stormed between him and his husband, Carver, refusing to be slowed by their questioning stares or their outstretched arms. He shoved his way past with Ollie trailing a few steps behind.

Van's voice boomed through the garage, echoing off the cement floors and metal ceiling. "Kyra! Get your pretty ass over here. Right. Fucking. *Now!*"

Ollie might not have known as much about Kyra as Van did, or even much about women in general, but he could guess that command wasn't going to work on her.

Not unless it was to draw her nearer so she could ram a drumstick up Van's ass while hoping he got the mother of all splinters from it.

Still, Ollie was on Team Van for this one. Why was Kyra taking stupid chances with her safety? Why not be frank with the head of security, whose literal job description it was to protect her?

Hell, Ollie had even told her he was going to rat her out if she didn't come clean herself. Yet she hadn't. Was that some kind of test? Because Ollie would pass it with flying colors.

Having lost the people closest to him in his life early on, he wasn't about to risk the wellbeing of any of his friends. Especially not Kyra. Because, let's face it. He was at least infatuated—if not half in love—with her, even if they never got the chance to share more than that single, solitary, stolen kiss.

She was strong, gorgeous, fun, and...maybe a little bit broken, like him.

Kyra also looked gorgeous when she emerged from the Hot Rides break room, where she'd been apparently been about to sample some of the fresh baked goods Devra had laid out there a little while ago. At least he assumed that's why she clutched a giant, gleaming knife in her fist as she marched out to meet them.

7

"What the fuck did you say?" Kyra waved a big-ass chef's knife toward Van, making him rethink his plan of attack. "Go ahead. Do it again, and I'll cut your balls off instead of kneeing them this time."

"Ooooo-kay." Wren plucked the polished metal from Kyra's hand. "No more sharp objects for you."

"Damn it," Kyra pouted, looking extra fine despite his anger and her annoyance. "He deserves it."

"Yeah, probably. But you'll thank me when you're falling asleep in your own bed instead of sharing a cell with Big Bertha." Wren took the weapon back to the break room where a crowd had been carving up one of Devra's creations. "Besides, I'm hungry. I need a piece of whatever this is. It looks amazing."

"Fine." Kyra rolled up the sleeves of the soft flannel shirt she wore open over a black tank and her favorite pair of ripped jeans. "Get me some too. I'm going to need it when I'm done with this asshole."

"Dude." Trevon shook his head at Van. "I felt bad for

59

you last time, but I'm kinda thinking I'd do the same thing if you were treating me like that."

Van winced and cupped his hands over his groin as he remembered how Kyra had taken him down. It didn't help that he flinched just enough to catch Ollie grinning from beside and slightly behind him, as if the guy was getting off on Kyra's bravado.

Ah, fuck it. He kind of was too. Except for one thing...

It might make Van a barbarian, but he'd do anything to keep Kyra from getting hurt. Why hadn't she told him she'd felt threatened? His temper spiked again. "I'm willing to take a hit if it means keeping her from getting killed by some psycho. I can't do my fucking job if I don't know that one of my clients is in danger."

Devra, Wren, and the guys all stared wide-eyed at Kyra then.

That was the line none of them would cross.

The Hot Rides gang had learned at least one thing from their friends the Hot Rods and the Powertools crew: they were fiercely protective of their own. When it came to looking after their by-choice family, there was no greater priority than keeping everyone whole.

Jordan shook his head. As a former special agent for the government and unofficial member of the band's security detail, he held his hands up, palms out. "You're on your own. I can't argue with him there."

Kyra's shoulders slumped and she glared beyond Van, most likely at Ollie.

"Hey, don't look at me like that. I told you I was going to say something if you didn't, and I keep my word. Unlike you..." Ollie's disappointment rang through the garage, drawing Van's attention.

He turned to look at the other man and was

surprised to see Ollie's face was flushed. A muscle twitched in his cheek. As far as Van knew, Ollie never got pissed off. It was kind of weird to see him without his signature smile and to hear the steely accusation in his voice.

Even still, Van didn't like anyone talking to Kyra in that tone. He pivoted toward Ollie, who put his arms up, his own fists clenched as if he'd go down swinging.

Van groaned. "I'm not going to hit you, dumbass. I just want to know what the fuck is going on."

"Oh. Right." Ollie stuffed his hands in the pockets of his faded black jeans and rocked back on his heels. Van was no dummy. This time Ollie had been ready, not only to absorb his blow, but to fight back.

Did Ollie feel that way about Kyra too? Sure, he'd walked away the night of their confrontation, but here they were again. Was this some elaborate scheme to steal her away now that he'd had a while to think about what he was missing out on?

Van wasn't about to roll the dice and find out. Not when Kyra was at stake.

"So?" he growled. If he didn't get answers soon, he might rip Ollie's head off despite the shaky cease-fire they'd reached outside.

"Ask her." Ollie jerked his chin toward Kyra, who cursed.

"Everyone is overreacting. It's nothing." She nibbled her lower lip and looked upward, as if she was thinking back on whatever had spooked her in the first place.

"Then it won't matter if you tell us about it," Wren interjected. "It's not like you to be evasive."

"Or nervous." Devra put her hand over Kyra's, where she was drumming her fingers furiously on her hip. The rest of their friends huddled around, as if they could defend her.

"I'm starting to think Van might have the right idea." Quinn cracked his knuckles. "Whose ass are we kicking and why?"

His brother, Roman, was right by his side, nodding. Whatever danger Kyra faced, at least they had plenty of people to keep an eye on her. Van's teeth unclenched, just enough for him to draw a deep breath and try to calm down.

"No one, yet. Honestly." Kyra dropped some of her attitude and crossed to Van. She planted her palms on his chest, instantly reducing his anxiety while ratcheting up an entirely different sort of tension within him. "I'm fine. Nothing crazy has happened. I think I was already so wound up about how we slept together and where fucking around would leave us that I felt an impending sense of doom. I got startled by something dumb, okay?"

A low murmur from the direction of their friends made Van sure their liaison was news to some of them. Yet everyone seemed supportive instead of acting like they had screwed up by crossing some invisible professional line. Hell, Kason—even though he was technically their boss— had encouraged him to take Kyra out to dinner, promising to stay in with Jordan nearly every night the past two weeks.

So why had Van still hesitated? Why was it so hard to tell her that he wanted a hell of a lot more than a bunk-breaking quickie, no matter how phenomenal that had been?

Oh, right. Because of their jobs and how messy it would be to spend every waking, and sleeping, moment together in a confined space if things fell apart.

As much as Van hated to hear Kyra say that the best sex of his life had triggered her anxiety, he sort of knew where she was coming from. Then again, things were pretty screwed up anyway. More so now that he realized she didn't trust him enough to care for her even if she'd let him inside her that one fateful afternoon.

"You were afraid so you called Ollie instead of telling *me* about it?" Van tried not to let that sting, but he'd take another knee to the nuts instead of her lack of confidence in him. He'd always had her best interests in mind, even when it meant denying himself something he craved desperately: her.

"No." Kyra shook her head. "Look, I went out for some fresh air and to clear my mind."

"Next time you need to do that, you take someone from my staff with you. It doesn't have to be me." Van tried not to seem petulant.

Without arguing, she gave a curt nod, which only made him sure she really had been frightened.

Damn it. Kyra didn't scare easily. Something was up.

"On the way back to the bus, I had a weird feeling. Like something was off. Or someone was watching me. I thought it was the guys playing one of their stupid pranks." She paused to clear her throat.

"Always trust your gut, Kyra," Jordan said quietly. "I've learned that the hard way. If you think something's up, it probably is. There's no harm in being cautious."

"Seriously, it wasn't a code red or anything. I came around a corner and—"

"Someone was there?" Van leaned in.

"Nah." Kyra shook her head. "There were flowers with a card addressed to me. And a balloon."

"Ever notice how fucking creepy balloons are?" Wren shuddered. "No, thanks."

"Good to know." Kason flashed a half-smile and tucked her close to his side.

"Hold up," Van locked in on Kyra. "That means someone *was* there. You just didn't see who it was."

"Oh, I know who it was." She couldn't have surprised him more.

"Who?" Had Ollie had the gifts delivered? Was that why she'd called him about them?

"Nobody important. I mean, just a fan. He's sent me stuff before and I'm pretty sure I've talked to him at some of our meet-and-greets." She brushed past that. "Anyway, Ollie happened to text me right when I got weirded out and it gave me the idea to call Hot Rods. You know, as a precaution, to talk to someone for a minute while I got the rest of the way back to the bus. I didn't know Ollie was in the garage or that he was going to answer the phone. And it's not my fault he's so damn good at reading people."

"It was pretty obvious you were freaking out," Ollie said.

"Not helping," she growled through clenched teeth before returning her focus to Van. "So settle your testosterone right down. I didn't specifically reach out to Ollie. In fact, if I'd had my way I...well, I wouldn't have told anyone. Okay?"

"Son of a bitch. That does *not* make me feel better." Van clasped her wrists in one of his hands. Although she seemed larger than life on stage and even off it, she wouldn't put up much of a fight against some crazed fan intent on overpowering her. Especially if she was caught off guard, away from him.

"What else aren't you telling anyone about?" Ollie

wondered as he approached. He stood to the side of Van and Kyra and reached out, cupping her chin so he could tilt her face toward him and look her directly in the eye.

Van caught the raised brows and interested glances from the rest of the Hot Rides. Only then did he realize what it looked like, with Kyra trapped between him and Ollie. And he couldn't say the idea didn't pique his curiosity. At least his dick perked up at the thought.

What would it be like to share a partner like that? To give them so much more than you could alone? What if...

He stopped short of imagining himself in bed with Ollie, or any other guy, for that matter.

Van dialed back in to the conversation in time to catch Kyra giving Ollie shit. "Nothing. I mean, I spilled my guts to you. Even about Van, although you took that a lot better than I expected, Mr. If-You're-Happy-I'm-Happy." She shot Ollie some serious side eye.

"Wait. What's that supposed to mean?" Ollie tipped his head. "Is it so bad to want the best for you, even if that's not me?"

"Not exactly. Though it would be nice to be wanted for once." Kyra shrugged one shoulder as if she hated to say so. She couldn't possibly be serious, could she?

"*For once*?" Ollie apparently couldn't believe what he was hearing either. "How can you have hundreds of men fawning over you every night, not to mention two guys who get in a brawl over your fine ass, and you still not realize how desirable you are?"

"Technically, I punched you. You didn't fight back." Van couldn't help but get another jab in.

"He's right, you know. You didn't fight for me. You let go. Despite what people say, I don't see anyone knocking down my door. Including you and Van."

"The guy knocked down the damn bed for you." Ollie grimaced.

Van's chest puffed up until Kyra rolled her eyes then continued, "And hasn't mentioned it since, acting like it never happened. Hell, I'm only talking about a date here, not marriage. Although I suppose I could accept Number One's proposal if I get desperate enough."

"Hold up. I'm lost." Ollie scrunched his eyes closed as if he was mentally rewinding her tirade like Van was, focusing on that Number One part.

Kyra smacked her palm into her forehead as if he, and probably every other guy she was ranting about, was impossibly dense. "Jesus, Ollie. That guy. The one who sends me stuff. He calls himself my Number One Fan. And in the card he left the other day, he asked me to marry him."

"Oh. That's pretty messed up." Ollie shook his head as Van racked his mind for some memory of this dickwad who was about to find himself on the band's blacklist. "Who proposes to someone they've taken selfies with a few times? He can't be serious, can he?"

"Uh, yeah. I actually think he is. Number One is a little...immature, is maybe the kindest way to say it." Kyra remembered thinking he made up for his lack of social skills with boundless enthusiasm.

"What else can you recall about him?" Van stood taller as he geared up to smash Number One like the bug he was becoming to Kyra.

"Not much. He's pretty young, probably not even able to drink yet. Scrawny. Harmless, I'm sure. He probably lives in his mother's basement and plays video games all day long. Not that there's anything wrong with that. He's just not...the kind of man I'd be afraid of." She shrugged, though her gaze shifted to the space between Van and Ollie. Were they the kind of men she feared? Why? She seemed to focus on something far in the distance when she said, "I was stressed out and let my imagination get the best of me. Can we please move on now?"

"I don't know." Ollie surprised Van when he didn't immediately capitulate to her demands. He cupped Kyra's upper arm and rubbed it. "Maybe you should let Van look into it some. I can still hear how shaky your voice was when I answered the phone."

"What the hell were the Hot Rides going to do from three states away?" Van growled. "Next time you have a problem, you call *me*. Got it?"

Ollie winced, as if he knew that tactic wouldn't work on Kyra. When it came to her safety at least, they were on the same team and had the same goals.

Sure enough, her eyes flashed and she glared at him. "I'll do whatever the hell I want. Just because I let you stick your cock in me doesn't mean you own me."

Ollie stepped between them before her jab could escalate to a full-on verbal assault. The other man kept his voice calm and soothing when he asked, "Is that why you didn't tell Van about whatever happened even though I asked you to? You were feeling like he had too much power over you, weren't you?"

"Yeah." She took a step closer to Ollie. "Exactly."

Huh. Okay, Van could learn a thing or two from the other guy. Try to understand where she's coming from instead of attacking her. Check. Or at least he'd try things that way, though he wasn't as skilled at this emotional shit as Ollie obviously was.

"Kyra, that's—" Van stopped short of denying it. He groaned as he implemented his shiny new resolution.

"Probably more accurate than I realized. I should have considered how avoiding you would come off when I was really just trying to figure out what to do next because when I'm near you I can't think at all. I'm sorry."

"You are?" Kyra seemed as floored as he was.

"Yes." Van glanced at Ollie, but he didn't care about the other man or the rest of their audience. They each had their issues. He'd had a front row seat as Kason, Wren, and Jordan worked through theirs. So it seemed only fair that they witnessed his. "I don't mean to be an asshole."

"It comes naturally, huh?" Ollie ribbed him.

Van shot the other guy the finger. "I'm doing my best to take care of you, even if I suck at it sometimes. If anything happened to you, it would crush me. And not only because it's my job to keep you safe, okay?"

She leaned into Ollie's hold and asked, "Because you want to fuck me again?"

"I'm going to go ahead and say yeah, he does," Quinn interjected.

"Stay out of it," Roman hissed.

Ollie groaned. Still, he didn't abandon Kyra when she needed his support to unearth her emotions even it had to be pretty much torture to know he was helping her get together—or *stay* together—with someone else.

Van rubbed the ache in his temples. How had life suddenly gotten so damn complicated? His dick was screaming hell yes, he did want to sleep with her again, but the more mature part of him, the parts above the belt, were shouting that he should show her he cared about more than only the physical aspects of their relationship and that he could still be professional. "No matter what happened between us before, my priority is to protect you."

Kyra deflated. "Right. It's what you get paid for. I guess that's part of it. I didn't want to remind you that we're coworkers above all else."

Kason spoke up. "For the record, you're adults. No one knows better than me that letting a job dictate who you can and can't be in a relationship with isn't the right answer. I don't have a problem with whatever you choose to do in your personal lives."

"Thanks, but it doesn't matter. It won't be happening again." Kyra stared at the floor.

Van suppressed his knee-jerk denial. This wasn't the time or place to state his case.

He couldn't allow himself to be distracted until he'd eliminated any threats to her.

So he stepped closer and tucked an errant curl behind Kyra's ear, hoping the gentle touch told her things he obviously wasn't good at communicating otherwise. She looked up at him once more. "I know for sure one thing that won't be repeating itself. Number One isn't going to bug you anymore. Maybe you're right and what happened was nothing. But just in case, I think I'll check out the storage unit where the PR company stashes the band's fan mail. Is it okay if I go through the stuff you've gotten lately and see what I can dig up?"

"Isn't that in L.A.?" Her eyes went wide.

"Yeah, so?" He spread his feet, prepared to stand firm.

Kyra sighed, the fight going out of her. "Sure. If you insist on wasting the whole week of break scouring bins full of signs and cards and letters for a figment of my imagination instead of spending time with me—"

He tried not to let his disappointment show, because yeah, he'd been hoping to get closer to her, not farther away, on their time off. "I do. I'm leaving."

Kyra's eyes lost some of their sparkle.

Van leaned in and kissed her on the forehead despite how awkwardly close that put him to Ollie. Too fucking bad if she didn't like the rest of the world knowing she'd slummed it by sleeping with him. He couldn't hide how he felt about her. Their friends weren't idiots either.

Kyra seemed unfazed by his show of affection. She deadpanned, "Knock yourself out."

"Want me to go with you?" Jordan offered immediately, though he winced as he did.

"No. You guys have been looking forward to your reunion for a few weeks now." Van smiled at Kason and Wren, who were flanking their lover. "Besides, I'll feel better knowing someone here is watching Kyra's back."

"I can take care of myself." She wrenched her face away from him, leaving him empty-handed. He stepped back, away from Ollie, and, therefore, Kyra.

"That doesn't mean I won't feel better if I know you've got friends nearby." Van sighed. He had no idea how to get through to her. To convince her that leaning on him, or anyone else, wasn't some indication that she was weak. Nor would it keep him from pursuing her as soon as he ensured Number One was as innocuous as she believed.

"I'm more than happy to watch every part of her for you." Ollie winked.

Van tried not to glower, but he wasn't very successful in the face of the other guy's deliberate provocation.

Kyra elbowed Ollie in the ribs as she smothered her grin behind the fingers of her other hand. "Quit it. Don't antagonize him."

"It's the truth." Ollie's gaze heated up as it sank in that Kyra would be spending a heck of a lot more time there, with him, at Hot Rides.

"She's right, you know. It's not a good idea to push me," Van snarled as he turned toward his unlikely ally and rival. "Like she told you, I've already seen every part of her and enjoyed the fuck out of them, too."

"So we're clear..." Kyra put her hand on her hip, making Van's dick hard as he remembered vividly what it had been like when she'd taken charge and ridden him. It made him want to show her exactly how reserved he'd been so far. But he wasn't likely to be able to let his true self loose around her or any woman. "Just because you and I hooked up once, it doesn't mean you're the boss of me. Hell, even if we were more than...whatever the hell it is we are...I'm not the sort of woman who takes well to being ordered around."

And that was the problem exactly, because Van enjoyed being in control. At least in the bedroom. Kyra was flat out telling him that they weren't a match, no matter how much it had appeared otherwise that day in her bunk.

"Got it." He nodded brusquely. "You're in charge of yourself. But you're also not stupid. So stay here, where you'll be protected. Whatever else happens, well, that's up to you. As long as you're safe, I'll be glad."

Kyra tipped her head as if she'd expected a fight. "You seriously don't give a shit if I shack up with Ollie in his teeny tiny campervan while you're away?"

"Hey, it's not that small," Ollie objected, making the Hot Rides guys crack up. Van was too concerned by whatever was going sideways with Kyra to worry about Ollie's wounded pride.

"It's only got one bed," she pointed out.

"That's a perk as far as I'm concerned," Ollie muttered under his breath.

"And you?" Kyra met Van's gaze, unblinking as she challenged him. "That's fine with you?"

Her scathing tone made it clear he'd said or done something wrong, but hell if he could figure out what. Did she want him to be possessive and jealous or not? Like always, she made his head spin. Maybe it was because he was so fucking attracted to her he couldn't think straight.

It was probably for the best that they take a break and put some distance between them, so they could decide where to go next and how to get there, hopefully together.

"You're a grown, independent woman." He tried to make himself clearer. "I loved every minute I spent inside you, and I'm ready to sign up for another go any time you're into it. But you're right. I don't own you. Do what you want, Kyra. You're my friend first. I care about you. All I want is for you to be whole and happy."

Liar. That wasn't *all* he cared about. But it was the bare minimum he could settle for.

"Oh." She seemed to shrink then, her sass evaporating.

It was hard for him to see her like that, especially knowing that somehow he was doing it to her. She'd be better off spending more time with Ollie. He seemed to get her. Always made her laugh and built her up like Van wanted to but couldn't seem to manage.

His voice was gruff when he said, "Don't worry, Kyra. I'm going to take care of this. Talk to you soon."

"You're leaving? Right now? You just got here." Devra looked to Quinn and then Trevon as if asking them to stop Van. Neither man did. Because if it were their wife in danger, they'd already be blazing out of Middletown on their motorcycles, hunting down the threat.

Van scanned the group of friends, nodding at Jordan and again at Ollie. He attempted a tight smile at Kyra, then spun on the heel of his boot and headed for his truck, lifting his hand to acknowledge their goodbyes and demands that he be careful.

He couldn't bear to look back and see Kyra, where he'd left her, in another man's very welcoming embrace.

8

The next day, Kyra emerged from the woods surrounding Hot Rides and wandered along the babbling brook toward the garage. Even in winter, with crispy leaves on the ground and clumps of ice left from the first real snow scattered here and there, it was peaceful, serene, and too damn quiet. She needed noise—like screaming fans, blaring music, and especially the beat of her sticks on the drums—to feel comfortable.

The whir of power tools would have to do for now.

Thankful for the gloves Ollie had lent her, she watched the fog of her breath dissipate. The hot chocolate Devra had promised would help thaw her. So she headed for the shop's break room.

At least with Devra and Wren around—plus the Hot Rods ladies sometimes, too—she had other badass women to hang out with, something she couldn't often say. Maybe Wren would teach her how to weld shit. With proper supervision, she probably wouldn't burn the place down.

It would be best if she did something—anything—in

addition to taking long, leisurely walks to bleed off her excess energy before spending another night crashed in Ollie's bed.

Oh yeah, that had happened.

Though to be honest, precisely *nothing* exciting had happened. Just actual sleeping.

Kyra had counted on having the excuse of freezing nighttime temperatures to justify a snuggle session at least. However, Ollie's home on wheels was surprisingly cozy, with a diesel heater and a plush down comforter that had thwarted her plans. She should have known Ollie wouldn't let Mr. Prickles get too chilled. He babied his hedgehog.

Kyra thought she might have sunk to new lows when she realized she'd grown envious of the critter.

Another night of lying next to Ollie might drive her insane. Neither of them had crossed over the perfectly friendly, and surprisingly wide, gap he'd left between their sides of the king-sized bed. So she'd lain there, cocooned in the comfort of his van, listening to his measured breathing and examining his surprisingly strong profile in the moonlight that flowed through the windows. At least Mr. Prickles had entertained her. His nocturnal rustling and antics, as he'd devoured his dinner and exercised on his running wheel, had kept her enthralled for more than a few sleepless hours. He was nearly as cute as his owner.

No matter how hard she'd tried to close her eyes and drift off, all she could think about was how Van had seemed so okay with letting her sleep around. And how very hands-off Ollie had been since Van had dropped her off and she had literally landed in his bed.

Was it wrong to be pissed that both of the men she

had crushes on were too damn gentlemanly for their own good? Or was it that neither truly craved her the way she desired each of them?

What was wrong with her? Confidence had never been something she'd struggled with before. Not in the male-dominated field she'd excelled in and not in any other aspect of her personal life. At least, not until both Van and Ollie had started keeping her at arm's length.

Even if Ollie hadn't been playing things cool with her, she wasn't sure what her goals were. At least this way she hadn't been forced into any difficult decisions.

For all Van said he didn't give a shit who she fucked, she figured that didn't mean he'd take her back if she chose someone else over him. Her problem was that she couldn't pick between them.

And that was exactly why she needed to find Devra and Wren for some advice.

While she never would have considered the possibility of being so greedy in the past, now that she'd seen firsthand how powerful and successful a non-traditional relationship could be, her mind kept racing to the taboo possibility of having her cake and eating it too.

What if she could find a way to be with both Ollie *and* Van instead of being torn between them?

Could she handle them both at once? Would they even be willing to consider an arrangement like that? If neither was all that interested in her to begin with, would a caveat like sharing her with another man scare them away entirely?

Kyra desperately needed some pointers on becoming a temptress when really she was just a tomboyish woman without much experience with the art of seduction. Was she capable of an advanced maneuver like initiating a threesome with two very different, very sexy men?

Would it be worth risking a shot at a relationship with one or the other to experience a single smoking night in bed with them both?

Um... Yeah, maybe.

Each guy had his own perks and downfalls. Things she loved about them and others she didn't as much.

Take Ollie, for example. He was so easy to talk to and quick to laugh with her. But although she'd given him plenty of green lights over the past few months, he seemed like he had been waiting for...something...to take things further. Even before she'd slept with Van.

The way he kept himself distant from the Hot Rides gave her reason to wonder if forming attachments was difficult or maybe impossible for him. The extra drama between them, in the form of one hulking and moody bodyguard, might be enough to scare him away despite the proof their panty-melting kiss had given that they would be absolute fire in bed together.

Had she killed his confidence when she'd wrenched out of his arms and stormed inside to rail at Van for ruining the moment? If so, sleeping with the guy certainly hadn't helped matters.

And Van, well, taking charge wasn't something he struggled with. But he could also be overbearing. Especially when he thought he knew what was best for her and that was keeping them apart.

Kyra was glad for the time and space to really be able to think without either of them influencing her with their potent pheromones.

When she strolled into the open bays with her hands jammed in the pockets of her charcoal pea coat, she was surprised to see two unfamiliar dudes hammering away at a sheet of metal, bashing it into a shape only they could envision. Despite the winter air pouring in from outside, they had their shirts off. Her eyes would have had to have been frozen shut to keep from noticing how damn impressive their physiques were.

One, the guy with curly chestnut hair and a full beard, had a massive tattoo of an eagle spanning his chest. The other had what seemed like acres of smooth tanned skin stretched over his cut muscles. Kyra nearly tripped over a compressor hose as she ogled the pair.

"Careful," Trevon cupped her elbow and steered her to safety. He leaned in so no one else would hear him teasing her. "Wouldn't want to break your neck while gawking at the new guys. Besides, Ollie might get even more jealous than he already is."

Kyra laughed and shook her head. She didn't bother to correct him about Ollie. Some hopelessly romantic part of her hoped it might be true even though he'd kept her firmly in the friend zone the night before. "Hey, I can't help it if you insist on filling this place with eye candy. Who are they?"

"Our new machinists. Hey, guys, come here a minute." Trevon waved them over. "I want you to meet Kyra."

When they saw Trevon gesturing at them, they shut down the machine, set aside their project, then stripped thick leather gloves off their big, skilled hands. They tucked them in the waistbands of their jeans, against abs glistening with sweat.

Whew. "I think I see why you call this place Hot Rides."

Trevon chuckled. "Not too shabby, huh?"

Kyra tried not to choke on her tongue as the duo

approached with matching, nearly predatory grins on their handsome faces. Suddenly starting to sweat, Kyra unbuttoned her jacket, took off her hat, and stuffed it into her pockets along with Ollie's gloves.

She barely resisted the urge to try to fluff her hair or arrange her unruly curls around her face so they were more flattering. What was wrong with her? Suddenly every man she met tripped her switch? Were her hormones going into overdrive as she neared thirty?

Or it could be she was meeting a whole new caliber of guys lately.

"What's up, Trevon?" the guy with the beard and chest tattoo asked.

"I want you to meet a friend of ours. This is Kyra Kado. She's the drummer for Kason Cox's band." Trevon's voice lost a little of its amused tone when he explained, "She's staying with Ollie for a few days while Van, Kason's head of security, checks into someone who's been harassing her. Since you're going to be around, I thought you should be informed of the situation."

The guys seemed to stand straighter at that, some sort of warrior instincts seeming to kick in. Damn it! That was exactly what she didn't need. Still, they remained polite, the bearded guy extending his hand. It swallowed hers when they shook. "Hey. Nice to meet you. I'm Walker. This is Dane."

He motioned with his head and then let go of her fingers so Dane could take up caressing her hand where his friend had left off. Maybe it was her previous train of thought about Ollie and Van and what it might like to be sandwiched between them, but her mind instantly went there with these two.

There was an invisible bond between them—in how

they moved, interacted, and played off each other—that made her sure they were a team. In the garage, for sure. Maybe in bed too.

"What's this about a stalker?" Walker asked.

Dane seemed to let his partner handle the talking, but he leaned in, observing her reactions closely as Walker interrogated her.

"It's not like that." Kyra shook her head as she waved her hands in front of her chest. Dane's eyes widened as he took in her own ink, which scrolled around her collarbones and dipped onto the top swells of her breasts. "Don't rile them up over nothing, Trevon."

"It's not *nothing*." He sent her a stern look that made her sure she was going to need to escape to her female friends soon or risk kneeing more overbearing men. Devra might not appreciate her smashing Trevon's balls as she'd said often how she'd like to have a family of her own someday.

Kyra almost wished the Hot Rides had laughed at Ollie's recounting of how she'd scurried back to the bus like a frightened mouse instead of taking her unease so seriously. That made it more real. More alarming. "I have a particularly devoted fan. I think he's harmless. Van is just making sure I'm right. That's all."

"I hope you are," Walker said. "But we're happy to keep an eye out, too. Dane and I were in the service together. We know how to take care of ourselves and those around us. Nothing will happen to you at Hot Rides."

"I know. And thanks." She smiled softly, touched by the kindness of these strangers. It was like that here in Middletown. If you were part of the gang, you had a readymade family waiting with open arms. It seemed like

Dane and Walker, and maybe her too, were going to fit right in.

With the serious business out of the way, Dane waded into the conversation. She greatly appreciated the diversion from topics she'd rather not think about. "Your tattoos are beautiful," he said as his eyes wandered along the most visible one toward her cleavage, highlighted by the low scoop neck of the cropped pink tank top she'd layered beneath another of her trusty flannel shirts. It had been worth the chill to see Ollie's expression as he'd taken in her bare midriff and the artwork peeking from beneath her shirt earlier that morning.

Dane was clearly wondering, as she prayed Ollie had, what she looked like without it on. Maybe she'd offer to give her van-mate a private exhibition of her full canvas later. It could be just the opening she needed.

Walker elbowed Dane. "I don't think those are tattooed. Quit it."

Kyra laughed and shook her head as she realized Dane's stare had landed on her boobs. Again, sad as it might be, it felt nice to know they'd noticed her as a woman and not only as a friend of the Hot Rides. Unlike Van, who acted so damn indifferent—other than when he'd let loose that solitary afternoon—and Ollie, who for some dumb reason was trying to behave around her despite Van's indifference about what they did together when he wasn't around. "They're not. Tattooed, I mean. Though they might be pierced."

She adored the way their eyes widened and the desire that flashed across even Walker's guarded face a moment before he asked, "You free for dinner?"

A shadow grew between them as someone

approached from the open bay door. "Sorry guys, she's eating with me."

Ollie.

Some part of Kyra was glad that he'd caught Dane and Walker ogling her, flirting, and generally raising her self-esteem. Unused to the mind games they'd all somehow found themselves playing, she found the constant tension exhausting. She had to do something about it, even if it ended in disaster.

"I am?" Kyra asked Ollie, trying not to glare. Why did he think he could keep her to himself if he didn't plan to make a move?

In the face of her ire, he surprised her. He didn't retreat this time. Instead, he stepped closer and took her hand in his. "Yep. I asked Devra to make us something special to share. You wouldn't want to ruin her efforts, would you?"

"I wouldn't miss out on Devra's cooking for anything." Kyra relented. It was impossible to stay annoyed when he was so damn nice and had put in extra effort for her. Somehow it didn't even piss her off that he'd assumed she'd eat with him. Hell, that's all she'd wanted—for him to take initiative. Give her some sign that he still felt like he had before their kiss, which had changed everything. At least with Van she no longer doubted he was physically attracted to her after he'd ravaged her, even if he regretted it later. "Thanks for going to the trouble to do something that sweet for me."

"I told Van I'd take care of you for him, and I meant it." He took his promises seriously. But still, she resented his motivation.

"I wish you'd do it because you want to, not because you were ordered to." Shit, she hadn't meant to say that out loud. But now that she had, it hung in the icy air like an icicle that could snap off and stab her through the heart at any moment.

"This sounds messy," Dane said, shaking his head and taking a step back. "I'm not into drama."

Kyra fought the urge to roll her eyes at him. "What relationship do you know of that's drama-free?"

"I guess that's why we only do hook-ups." Dane shrugged.

"*We* as in, we separately hook up with women, or do you mean *we* hook up with each other, or like *we* hook up with women together?" Kyra figured she'd come this far. Might as well stuff her foot *allllll* the way down her throat. Ollie and Trevon tried to look like they weren't paying rapt attention but she knew they were curious, too, even if she was the only one rude enough to ask point blank.

Dane and Walker didn't seem to mind being frank. They fist bumped each other before Walker said, "Whatever we feel like that night. But let's just say we accepted Quinn's job offers because we thought we might fit in pretty well around here."

Trevon grinned, making Kyra realize that although he adored his wife and their husband, even he was sometimes still unsure of how the world would treat them because of their unconditional love. Without thinking about it too much, she leaned over and hugged him.

Ollie chuckled. "Well, shit. If it's good enough for all of you, maybe that's what I should be looking for too."

Say what?

Kyra was glad she was hanging on to Trevon or she might have landed flat on her ass on the garage floor.

9

Kyra eyed Walker and Dane as they drifted back to work at their station, as if they hadn't been the catalyst for the explosion that had just blown her mind. If they were as seamless of a team in bed as they were in the garage, she envied the women they shared.

"I'll catch up with you guys later. Gotta finish..." Trevon mumbled something or other that made Kyra pretty sure he had noticed the charge in the air and was being nice enough to give her and Ollie some room to figure out what to do about it.

Ollie cleared his throat. When she turned to face him, trying to shove her dirty thoughts aside, he leaned in and murmured. "Is that something you're into? Would you want me more if I was a package deal?"

She tried not to gasp as the images of him and Van making love to her rushed back into her mind. After all, they were the two guys she'd lusted after lately. And they complemented each other in so many ways.

Still, she didn't want Ollie to get the wrong idea. She

knew what it was like to never feel good enough. The thought of hurting him like that was one of the things still holding her back when it felt like the universe, their friends, and her own desires kept nudging them in that direction. "You're plenty on your own, Ollie. For me or any woman."

He smiled then, serious for once. "Thanks."

"But I'd be lying if I said the idea isn't hot as hell." She fanned her face despite winter creeping into the garage behind them. "I mean, haven't you ever thought about having a threesome with two women?"

"Uh..." Something about the way he hesitated tipped her off.

"Hang on. Have you *had* a threesome before?" Kyra looked around to make sure no one had overheard her outburst, then dragged him from the shop.

This wasn't a discussion she was ready to have in front of an audience, even if it was composed of the least judgmental people she'd met, who could also relate to being involved in complicated relationships. She led Ollie to his campervan, dashing through the flurries that had begun to drift down around them.

Somehow, it seemed easier to talk to him inside his tiny home. It was cozy and comforting and made her feel like a carefree kid on a summer trip. Almost like the world outside didn't exist and the repercussions for what they were toying with weren't so damn drastic.

Once inside, she stripped off her boots and outerwear before resting her hip against the counter of his kitchenette. A few feet beyond was his bed, and in the other direction the tiny bathroom, which was essentially a shower stall with a composting toilet inside. Both the driver and passenger seats were on swivel bases and currently rotated so there was a seating area up front, complete with bean bag foot rests and a compact table on a removable pole inserted between them.

Ollie had thought of nearly everything. Though the space was tight, each inch was optimized and useful. Quinn and Eli had been hounding him lately to put together a business plan that would allow the Hot Rods and Hot Rides to add van renovations and build-outs to their menu of services. He'd be perfect to head up that operation if he ever chose to abandon his salvage runs.

Kyra wiggled her fingers at Mr. Prickles, who blinked as if scolding her for her hesitation. If she balked now, they'd never discuss the possibilities hanging between them. As soon as Ollie shut the door, hung up his coat, and turned toward her, she took a deep breath and went for it.

"So..." she asked again. "You've had two women before?"

"Yup." He shrugged as if it wasn't a big deal. He wasn't bragging, simply telling her what she'd asked about. "It wasn't anything serious. A hell of a lot of fun, though. I never made it to college, but I did once wrangle an invite to a random frat party that got kind of wild."

"I'd think our definition of *kind of* might be different." Kyra gaped.

He was so unassuming. The idea of him handily pleasing not only one but two women at the same time did something to her. Made her want to find out what those lucky ladies had already learned about him and what he was like in bed.

Would they laugh as they tangled in the sheets? Would he make her feel as comfortable and secure as he did when they were in separate states watching the same videos online and making snarky comments about them over the phone late at night? Or would it be totally different once his erotic side, one she might not know as well yet, was unleashed?

"Is *that* something you'd be into?" Ollie rubbed his chin. "I could probably find one of their numbers..."

Kyra figured she owed him some confessing of her own. "Been there, done that. Didn't get any damn T-shirt, though."

Now it was Ollie's turn for some rapid mind expansion. His brows rose as he considered the secret she'd shared, one she'd never told anyone, not even Van. He took a step forward as if the knowledge drew him to her instead of scaring him away. It was like that night behind the arena, when she'd gotten a glimpse of the man he kept so tightly under wraps. The one who'd taken what they both wanted in that unforgettable moment. "That's so sexy, Kyra. Was it a serious relationship?"

"No, it was kind of like you said. I mean, I didn't go to college either. But being young and on the road with bands full of up-and-coming musicians who had more hormones than brains, I was around plenty of parties. One night this woman I'd been hanging out with— dancing and drinking with—came on to me. It felt worldly and, in a weird way that I now realize was probably completely false, safer than hooking up with some random guy that night. She was patient and kind and, yeah, hot as hell. I don't think it's what I want all the time, but I'd do it again if the right situation presented itself." Kyra glanced up at him from beneath lowered lashes then, hoping that didn't change his opinion of her too much.

The windows of the campervan were already steaming

up from their breath. She averted her gaze and tracked a bead of condensation as it ran down the window, drawing a brighter line through the haze in its wake.

When Ollie didn't say anything, but studied her as intently as she was monitoring the progress of water droplets on the glass, she tried to shrug it off. "I guess it's kind of like Dane and Walker said. What's the harm in a good old-fashioned hook up every once in a while, right?"

Except that sounded like she was hitting on him. Shit!

Wait...was she? Kyra shifted, uncomfortably aware of what her wicked thoughts and naughty memories were doing to her body.

"I suppose. If it's not going to screw up other stuff like your ability to be friends with someone." Ollie took another step closer, trapping her against his bed, and she realized they were wandering into dangerous territory. "Do you think it's worth the risk for a few orgasms?"

Kyra nearly choked on her tongue as she wondered if he was asking hypothetically or because he planned to do something about it if she said yes. Of course, that kept her from responding fast enough.

Ollie retreated a few steps. "Yeah, me either."

He combed his fingers through his wavy hair as he stared at the ceiling and blew out a deep breath.

"Really? Are you sure? Because I was going to say..." Kyra knew that once she admitted it, she couldn't take it back. It would be right there, between them, changing everything.

"What?" He cut his stare to her.

"Yes. I was going to say yes, it's worth taking a gamble." Kyra couldn't help but think of the climaxes Van had pushed her to. They'd wrecked something inside her as surely as they had her bunk on the bus. "But if you don't think so, then maybe you've never had good enough orgasms."

Suddenly she wanted very much to obliterate Ollie's past experiences and the limits of what he'd thought was possible.

Had anyone ever done that for him?

Freezing rain interspersed with flurries pinged on the roof. It didn't matter, it wouldn't last long. The heat that began to radiate from them would melt it in an instant. If they didn't do something about it soon, she was going to have to go outside naked to cool down.

Ollie wrapped his hands around her waist and boosted her onto his elevated bed, which allowed for storage and a spot to stow the refrigerator underneath. He was nimble and surprisingly aggressive as he followed her up, pressing her shoulders into the mattress.

Kyra fed off his energy, rolling and taking him to his back so she could straddle him. She planted her hands on his chest, feeling powerful and free in a way she hadn't with Van, who nearly always overwhelmed her.

Leaning in, she murmured against Ollie's lips, humming when his hands grabbed her ass and held her tight to his body so she couldn't mistake the ridge of his arousal between her thighs. "Will you let me fix that for you? I mean, I know I'm only one woman, not two, but I'm very motivated..."

"One of you is enough." He echoed her earlier sentiment and made her heart swell.

His irresistible blend of sweet and sexy nearly inspired her to run across the lawn and beg Devra or Wren to lend a hand in ravishing him. Except although Wren was openly poly, she was also in a committed relationship with Kason and Jordan, same as Devra was with Trevon and Quinn.

So Kyra would have to perform solo.

This time she sealed her mouth over his, taking full responsibility for what would happen because of their actions. Both in bed together, and out of it...after.

She wasn't going to think about that.

Not then, when endorphins got her high on him.

Kyra hadn't gotten her fill of him that night they'd been interrupted. She intended to make up for it. Her lips glided across his, making them both hold their breath as they stared into each other's eyes. Ollie took the opportunity to run his hands upward. He tugged the open flannel shirt from her shoulders and dragged it down her arms, pinning them behind her for a moment or two before freeing her.

Then he was back, his fingers toying with the exposed skin of her lower back and his thumbs brushing above her hip bones and below the loose lower hem of her cropped tank. She shivered and moaned into his parted mouth.

Kissing him was easy. It wasn't about power plays or proving something to each other. It was mutual joy and pure pleasure. Exactly what she needed.

If it was this good to taste him, to tease his tongue with hers and smile against his seeking mouth, she couldn't wait to go further.

Kyra broke them apart barely long enough to rid herself of her tank and the pink satin bra she'd had on beneath it. Ollie flopped onto the bed, his expression one of awe and reverence. It pumped her confidence through the roof. His hands came up then, to cup her breasts, making her nipples tighten against his palms.

He held her, squeezed her, and toyed with the metal bars there until her eyes drifted shut.

So she didn't see him lunge upward.

Ollie wrapped one arm around her waist then flipped her, making her laugh as she crashed into the pile of pillows he used to convert his bed into a recliner when he lounged there, as they had while watching videos in bed that morning. "Damn, Kyra. You're gorgeous. I want to see all of you. Taste all of you. Take all of you."

Oh. Okay, then. Her heart skipped a beat because she believed him.

Ollie wasn't the kind of guy who'd say whatever it took to get in her pants. Besides, the raw truth in his appreciative gaze thawed her, making her melt.

She nodded, unable to say anything coherent. Especially when he dove between her thighs, tucked his fingers in the waistband of her jeans, then tugged the button open with his teeth. He yanked, pulling them down fast enough that the cool air shocked her core.

He tossed the denim over his shoulder. It landed over Mr. Prickles' cage. Probably for the best if the hedgehog didn't see what they were about to do.

Then Kyra was left with only a scrap of pink lace separating her from Ollie.

Even that was too much.

She squirmed, trying to rid herself of the material.

Ollie swallowed hard as his gaze scanned her nearly nude body, on display for him and ready for anything he wanted to try next. Unlike Van, he didn't rush. Instead, his finger traced the intersection of her skin and the silk. "You're so soft. I could touch you all day."

"You could, but then I'd go crazy." She was about to

beg as it was. "Take your clothes off. I want to see you and touch you, too."

He nodded, then made quick work of it, ripping open the snaps of his long-sleeved, black shirt to put his surprisingly cut yet lean torso on display while he concentrated on getting rid of his socks and pants. It was a little awkward in the limited space, but he didn't get tripped up by that, instead chuckling at their predicament and how desperate they were for each other.

Kyra knew right then. Sex with Ollie would be remarkable. It would be like the world's best comfort food, nourishing her soul along with her body.

And she couldn't wait another moment to experience it.

Unfortunately, that's exactly when Ollie hesitated. He knelt on the bed beside her, his ass resting on his heels and his hands palms up on either knee.

His cock, hard and ready, made it clear it wasn't because he didn't find her attractive.

"You're sure?" Ollie asked, giving her a chance even then to change her mind. "If we do this, it's done. I'm not going to hide it from Van or anyone else."

"I wouldn't ask you to." Something about him called to Kyra, deep inside, to the parts of her that weren't as secure as she'd like or as confident as she acted. It also gave her the courage to take charge. Whereas with Van, she'd laid back and taken what he'd given her, with Ollie...she wanted to be the person who could do that for him. "I'm positive. I can't say what will happen tomorrow, but for right now—"

"That's all I'm concerned about." He reached out and put his hand on the side of her neck, drawing her to him for another kiss. She didn't stop there this time.

Kyra kissed along his jaw and then lower, dragging her teeth down the exposed length of his neck. That he trusted her so much, gave her free rein, it encouraged her to deserve his faith. To make whatever they had incredible while it lasted.

She sank lower while he rose up as if he couldn't bear to stay mostly seated. He knelt on the bed while she went onto all fours. Kyra licked a meandering path down the center of his chest and abs, tempted to pause and knead the muscles flexing there in response to her every touch.

Right before she reached his navel, she teased him. "Tell me what it was like with two women. I have to know what I'm up against."

Though he chuckled, he didn't play along. "What if I tell you about something else instead?"

"Like what?" She glanced up, refusing to be distracted for long. So she saw the immense relief and the renewed desire that flashed across his face when her palm dragged along his inner thigh until she cradled his balls in her palm.

It was heady to witness the impact she had on him. A pearl of precome appeared at the tip of his erection. She licked it from him, grinning when he cursed. It took him a few seconds to recover, during which she stroked him with long, slow passes of her hand on his cock.

She couldn't wait to feel him moving within her to the rhythm that would become uniquely theirs. Still, he had some tricks of his own remaining.

"You should ask me if I've ever been with another guy." His hips jutted forward, making it impossible to ignore how his hard-on stiffened and grew beneath her caresses. Damn, he was more impressive than she'd expected.

Kyra measured his length with her fingers, loving the heat and weight of him in her hand.

"Have you done it?" she asked, somewhat surprised, though she supposed she shouldn't have been. Simply because he'd always been interested in her didn't mean he wasn't interested in others—similar to her or not—too.

He nodded. "Hell yes. It's been a while, but I'm willing to experiment and try things at least once. Or...more than once, if I end up liking it."

"Ollie, damn." She panted. "That's so sexy."

"No offense, but there's nothing quite like a blowjob from another man. At least not according to my old roomie." Ollie shrugged. "That guy who invited me to the frat party? We shared a shitty college-town apartment while he was in school. There were a few times I couldn't pay my rent and he offered me an alternate arrangement."

"You did what you had to in order to survive." She kissed his hip, wishing he didn't always seem so damn alone. After today, she swore he would never be again.

They were more than friends. It had been coming for a while.

It was time she acknowledged that fact. "No matter what happens, Ollie, I need you to understand I'll always be here for you. Okay?"

He grimaced. "Thanks, but don't feel bad for me or some shit. Sorry, it's hard to think with you...doing that. I made it sound sleazier than it was. He liked it, and so did I. At least on a physical level. We didn't have any deeper connection than that. And so when he graduated, we went our separate ways."

"Is that what you'll say about me someday?" She cleared her throat, afraid of the answer.

Ollie reached down and cupped her chin in his hand.

He lifted until she couldn't look anywhere but deep into his warm, rich eyes. "Never. I've never felt like this about someone before. You get me. You're...so much more than a person I crossed paths with once."

Good enough for her. Kyra evaded his hold and opened her mouth. She took him inside and glided down his shaft, using her tongue to lave the underside of his erection until he nudged the back of her throat.

"Fuck!" He buried his fingers in her hair, holding her there. She had a feeling it wasn't because he was trying to trap her but because if she moved, he might lose control.

Now that was something she'd like to see.

When he relaxed his hold, Kyra sucked him, bobbing over him, challenging herself to take more of him each time she went down. Meanwhile, her body began to ache. She needed to feel him, inside her, soon, taking away her doubts and emptiness, replacing it with...him.

"Enough." He tapped her cheek with one finger, drawing her from her mission to prove one mouth could be better than two.

Had she failed?

The flush spreading across his chest and up to his cheeks said she hadn't.

"I'm not going to be satisfied until I'm buried in you." He smiled at her then, some of his gentle affability returning. "Will you finally let me in, Kyra?"

Had she been the one keeping them apart?

Yeah, she had. All the nights they'd spent talking on the phone, all the texts, the flirty conversations, the movie nights they'd had—even some with Van—while Kason had been visiting with Wren and Jordan. They'd all led to this moment.

They'd forged a bond she was tired of denying.

Kyra bit her lip and nodded. She pulled off him and held up her hand. He took it. Together they tumbled onto the bed, ending up on their sides, facing each other. Neither of them on top and neither on the bottom. They were equals in a way she never experienced with Van or any other partner.

Ollie caressed her from her shoulder, down her arm, and then across her hip. He smiled as he rubbed his nose against hers before indulging in another sweet kiss. But as they made out and their chests pressed together, stealing her breath, the rest of them aligned as well.

Soon his cock was there, tucked between her legs, making her squirm to fit him better.

They strained together, rocking and kissing. It was unlike any other sexual encounter—with a man or woman—she'd had in her life.

This was something more than scratching an itch.

When the blunt tip of his cock edged the barest bit inside her, they both gasped and froze.

Staring into each other's eyes, they wrapped their arms around each other and clung, forcing their bodies to join as tightly together as she suspected their spirits also had.

As he spread her open and connected them, Kyra felt free. To express herself, to openly communicate her elation and pleasure, and even to share her doubts and fears, knowing he'd never judge her.

Ollie moved inside her, wrapping her knee in his hand and lifting it so he had a wider range of motion. Kyra clung to him, rocking her hips to meet him halfway. Damn.

Whether it was the position or Ollie himself, she had never felt anything like this before.

Sex with Van had been an explosion of desire pent up too long between two people who didn't know any other way to dissolve the mounting tension they triggered in each other.

This was...

Everything else. Liquid grace and patience and sensual exploration.

Kyra blinked as she refocused on Ollie's face. He smiled and asked, "What are you thinking? Do you want me to stop?"

"God, no!" She clutched his shoulders, hoping she didn't leave permanent dents there.

"Then what?" he asked. "I can see something's on your mind. Tell me so you can let go of it and feel."

"Well..." She cleared her throat before blurting, "If you already had a threesome for fun, does that mean you'd do it with someone you cared about? Would you get off on sharing me with someone else? Or would you be jealous?"

"Of Van, you mean?" Ollie paused, then fucked deeper on his next thrust. He locked within her before answering. "I think that could take things to a whole new level. Because as much as I care about you, I know he does too. I'd like to watch someone else get you off, maybe have some help to ensure you're enjoying it when we make love."

Was that what they were doing? Kyra thought it might be the first time she'd ever done that and not just had sex with someone. Everything about their encounter was smooth and slow like he was pouring melted pleasure over them where they lay clasped together.

It was amplifying her arousal to hear him say these

things, so taboo and yet earnest, as if it was the most natural thing in the world.

"You don't need any help, Ollie." She sighed as he nudged her higher, closer to coming. "You're doing a damn fine job on your own."

"Okay, then maybe it would be for my benefit too." He closed his eyes and his motions stuttered.

Until she kissed him and whispered, "Now *you* tell *me*. How so?"

The thought that they really both might need the same things made her quiver around him. When her pussy hugged him tighter, he groaned. Then the truth fell from his parted lips. "Because I need help getting out of my head so I don't freak out about...shit I don't want to think about right now. Van is perfect for that and I know he'd never let anything bad happen to you because of me."

"Why do you think us being together would make something bad happen to me?" Kyra moaned when he rubbed against a sensitive spot inside her. It certainly felt amazing to her.

"Because it always does to people I love." Ollie didn't give her a chance to ask any clarifying questions and to be honest, her capacity for deep thoughts was rapidly evaporating.

He smothered her in a bear hug and crushed his mouth to hers, encouraging her to grind herself on him as they came together over and over.

Ripples of ecstasy expanded from every place they made contact, motivating Kyra to give all of herself to ensuring Ollie felt the same. She hooked her leg around his hip, clasped his head to hers, and fed him every cry of rapture he triggered.

She tightened gradually around him until the pressure, though exquisite, was too much to bear.

"Kyra, I can't last much longer." He bit her lower lip then sucked on it as his hips worked, drilling him deep within her.

"You don't have to, Ollie." Kyra rested her forehead on his and gasped as she began to fall with him. "I'm with you."

He shuddered and called her name as he flooded her with his heat and desire. The sensation gave her the final boost she needed, along with his pelvis tapping her clit.

Kyra came around him, milking him dry with the corresponding spasms of her own body.

She couldn't say how long they flew together, but she was content to lie there and rub up against him as they both savored every last moment of bliss.

And when it was over, the silence they shared was every bit as sacred.

Together, they listened to the patter of the icy precipitation bouncing off the roof of Ollie's home. A bone-deep sense she was welcome to make it her own changed something within her. She hadn't had that sense of security since she was a kid, since before she realized that her parents were unusual and not everyone lived their vagabond lifestyle.

What would it be like to have a place that was hers instead of an assigned sleeping spot for the drummer of whatever band she was working for at the moment? Sure, she'd been with Kason for nearly seven years now. Wildly successful ones, where she and Kason and Van and the rest of the guys had become like a surrogate family. But this...this was different.

Because unlike Van, Ollie was claiming her as his own. Or at least she thought he might be.

His lids were heavy when he finally opened them to smile across at her. "That was incredible, Kyra."

"It was." She grinned back, finally completely relaxed in his company. "I can't wait to do it again. I mean, if that's what you're thinking too—"

"I'm sure as hell not planning on forgetting it happened." He looked at her as if she was nuts, but that's exactly what Van had done, despite the way they'd come together, more intensely though maybe less emotionally binding in their urgency.

"Good. Me either." She kissed him softly.

"Can we figure out how to make this work for more than a night or two or ten?" Ollie ran one fingertip along her eyebrow, then tucked a curl behind her ear.

"It might take a minute, but I think so." She needed to believe that was true. Kyra hadn't wanted anything so badly since Kason's old manager had announced they'd been nominated for the best new artist Grammy they'd taken home years ago.

There was only one major hurdle they needed to make it over first.

She groaned, "So who's going to break it to Van?"

10

"Break it to Van that we had sex?" Ollie winced. "I will, as long as it's from more than an arm's length away."

Kyra chuckled at that. "Smart. But no, I mean, who's going to tell him that we talked about getting it on with him while we fucked?"

"In that case, I think he'd take it better coming from you." Ollie rubbed his eyes, then let his hands fall. "Was that weird? It probably was. Sorry."

"I think I brought it up." Kyra smiled sheepishly. "So if it was, I take the blame. But no, Ollie, nothing about this feels wrong to me. It feels natural and...wonderful."

"To me too." He squeezed her, sighing when she nuzzled his chin and settled against his chest.

Kyra drew the fluffy duvet over them and snuggled up against Ollie's side. Though he didn't have Van's bulk, his honed muscles were impossible to miss. He had zero body fat, though he didn't seem to mind hers. His fingers tested her hips and ran over her curves as they idly traveled across her.

Kyra laid her head on his chest and listened to him breathing as his heart settled down. She could swear it was beating in sync with her own.

Ollie was a world-class cuddler. Nestled in his bed, with the wintry mix tapping a steady beat above them, she drifted off. It was easy to dismiss the real reason she'd come back to Hot Rides and pretend that they were forging a genuine and lasting bond. Those were dangerous thoughts. Still, she couldn't help but dream about what could be.

Kyra sighed while Ollie stroked her hair and drew a figure eight on her back and shoulders. Being with him was easy and so damn satisfying, she wasn't sure she would ever get tired of playing around with him.

He kissed her temple, burrowed into his pillows, then held her close.

They must have dozed, intertwined, for quite a while because the next thing Kyra knew, Devra was banging on the side of the campervan. "Hurry up! Open the door. This dish is heavy, and hot. Kind of like it sounded you two were earlier."

Ah, shit. There was no point in pretending she was wrong. Besides, Kyra's stomach rumbled.

She scooted out of Ollie's bed and threw one of his soft, worn henleys on. Even though she thought of him as short compared to Van and the rest of the Hot Rides, it still hung nearly to her knees. She jogged the couple of steps to the side door of the camper van as Ollie sat up and stretched. His hair was adorably mussed and he seemed even more out of it than she felt.

When she opened the sliding panel, and Devra popped inside—carrying something that smelled incredible—Kyra glanced at Ollie, who shook his head like a dog emerging from a lake. He scrubbed his knuckles over his eyes then realized he was on full display to not only her but Devra as well.

"Ah, shit. Sorry." He grabbed a pillow and held it over his lap.

"Don't be on my account." Devra grinned. "You're pretty sexy when you're worn out."

He chuckled bashfully, then said, "Thanks. I think."

"Are you ready for Trevon and Quinn to help me bring in the rest?" Devra asked them both.

"*The rest?*" Kyra glanced at her friend, then at Ollie. "This is a ton of food!"

"The guys are hoping there will be leftovers when you're finished." Devra chuckled. "There's plenty more coming. You two sit back and let us bring you a romantic dinner in bed."

"I can't say I've ever had that experience before, but I'm open to any number of firsts." Kyra winked over her shoulder at Ollie, who was quick to laugh as always.

He smirked as he patted the bed beside him. "Who are we to let her hard work go unappreciated? Amiright?"

"Absolutely!" Kyra dashed past Mr. Prickles' cage and sprang onto the bed, worming until she was sitting crisscross applesauce in front of him, carefully tucking his shirt between her legs.

"If that shirt wasn't already my favorite, it would be now." He leaned in and dropped an easy, familiar kiss on her lips as he fussed with the collar.

It felt kind of weird to let Devra, Quinn, and Trevon set up the campervan. With all five of them in the limited space, there wouldn't have been room for her or Ollie to help even if they'd been banned from doing so. In no time, trays of appetizers, covered dishes holding entrees, and a tiered stand dotted with mini desserts had been set out on the bed and the kitchenette counter, all within reach of her and Ollie.

There was even a tiny bowl with the odds and ends of some vegetables for Mr. Prickles.

In addition, Devra set out several chrysanthemums in full bloom, a bottle of wine chilling in a bucket, and began to scatter buttery yellow candles in mason jars on the remaining counter space. Ollie tensed visibly.

"You okay?" Kyra asked softly, putting her hand on the bunched muscles of his thigh.

"Uh, yeah. I just..." When Devra went to light the candles, he flinched.

Quinn noticed it too. He put his hand over Devra's, preventing her from striking the match, then said, "Let's leave them some counter space for the dirty dishes, huh?"

His wife shot him a questioning glance but didn't argue when he shook his head and cut his eyes toward Ollie, who was gradually relaxing again although he'd turned somewhat ashen.

Trevon covered for whatever had gone wrong. He gathered up the candles in his arms and leapt down from the campervan. "I'll take these back to the house for you, babe. Time to leave them alone to enjoy all your hard work."

Devra nodded. "I hope you have a great dinner. It seems to me like you have a lot to celebrate."

"We will and we do. Thank you. You went way above and beyond what we talked about." Ollie blew her a kiss, his usual self reappearing from under the dark cloud that had briefly obscured his perpetually sunny disposition.

"I wanted to make sure it's special. For you both." She

leaned in and wrapped an arm around each of them, hugging them tight before turning to go.

"Should we assume that if the campervan's a-rockin'..." Quinn teased as he took Devra's hand and led her to the door.

"I'm going to be too full to have sex after this." Kyra snorted. "Don't think I'm not going to try every single one of those desserts."

"Well shit, then I'm taking this stuff back!" Devra pretended to scoop up a dish but Quinn dragged her away, both of them cracking up as they tumbled into the brisk evening air.

"Good night. Have fun!" Quinn yelled as he slammed the door.

Kyra exchanged a glance with Ollie and they burst out laughing. When the fit died down, they were left with each other and a gorgeous date, set up by the man she was no longer thinking of as a friend, and his friends. He wasn't afraid to tell everyone he knew that he was interested in her and that he planned to do something about it.

That was a refreshing change.

"Thank you for arranging this." She leaned in and kissed him again with a brush of their lips that lingered longer this time. If there weren't trays and hot food everywhere, they might have had each other for an appetizer.

While they ate, they talked about everything and nothing, bouncing between not-so-serious topics like who they thought would be eliminated next from their favorite reality TV show to some ideas she had for upcoming stage costumes. Suddenly, she was feeling like she might like to be bolder with her style choices.

Ollie made her feel like that, shiny and as if she maybe wouldn't mind drawing a little more attention to herself sometimes. At least if it felt as good as it did when he was looking at her like he was right then. Like she was somehow amazing to him when she was simply being herself.

"Damn it, I wanted to try them all." Kyra pouted when she realized there was no way she could stuff another dessert into her stomach.

"Here, have a bite of mine." He held out some sort of chocolate cake to her and she decided she'd make room.

He cupped his hand under her chin to keep crumbs out of the bed as she took a taste of the decadent treat and hummed. It was worth it, even if she couldn't move for a week.

Without thinking, she wrapped her lips around his index finger and thumb, then sucked them clean.

"Damn." His eyes turned molten as he slumped against the cushions. "If I wasn't about to pop, I'd tell you to keep doing that."

Kyra chuckled, because she knew exactly how he felt. Stuffed, completely satisfied, and more relaxed than she could remember being...maybe ever... Kyra laid her head on Ollie's shoulder and sighed.

"Is that a happy sigh or a sad sigh?" he asked, while stacking their dishes and trays on the kitchen counter. He cleaned his hands on a black linen napkin before putting his arm around her and resting the side of his face on top of her head.

How could she answer without hurting his feelings? Being honest was the only thing she knew how to do. "Definitely not sad. Relieved. And maybe a tiny bit anxious."

"Why so?" He stroked her hair, telling her with his touch that it was okay to have mixed feelings.

"Because for right now I'm content. And you're not kicking me out or making me feel like what we shared was just a temporary madness. Some kind of slipup you're going to regret in the morning."

He angled his chin down so he could kiss her forehead. "Definitely not. No matter what happens tomorrow, today will always be one of the best days of my life. Thank you for that."

"Same, Ollie. Seriously. It's just that all the stuff I feel for Van is still there in the background, too. You know? I'm kind of mad at myself that I can't make it go away when he obviously doesn't want this with me and you're here offering me everything I've needed from him but was missing." Kyra splayed her hand on Ollie's warm, steady chest, drawing on his calm to keep her from getting upset.

"I hate to say this... But I will because I care about you more than I want to keep you to myself." He whispered, "I think Van would like to give you the same things, but he doesn't know how. It's harder for him because you work together and I think it really hurt him that you didn't confide in him about the stalker. You hit him where he's the most confident: in his ability and desire to protect you. Even if he thinks it's from himself. And if he can't even be sure about that, how could he be certain he's the right man to do more than the basics, like pleasing you and being all the other things a lover should be to their partner?"

Kyra pushed up so she could stare into Ollie's eyes. Was he seriously making a case for Van?

What the hell?

And did that piss her off because he was right? Had

she fucked with Van's head without even meaning to? Shit. Probably.

Ollie drew her back down and cradled her against his body. "Listen to what I'm saying, please. I'm here. I'm not going anywhere. And I want you to stay with me. But if there's any chance for this to become something that lasts, we've got to handle the rest too."

"I know we do. And what you're saying makes sense. I did screw up. I just hope it's not too late to fix it." Kyra groaned. "I mean, if that's what you want too."

"I want you. And I want you to be as happy as possible. I've seen you with Van. You have a connection that goes beyond friendship. I came into this knowing that. So I'm ready for whatever happens." Ollie hesitated then said, "I don't want to act like it's going to be easy, but...I think Van made it clear the other day that he knows what's up too, even if he doesn't know how to handle it. So no, I don't think it's too late. This is complicated. It's not going to be resolved tonight. Why don't you relax and let me hold you while I can? I don't want to let worrying about the future and things out of our control ruin what time I can enjoy spending with you."

"You're pretty smart, Ollie." She sighed again, entirely at ease this time, and nuzzled his throat.

"I know." He grinned.

His arm curled around her waist. True to his word, as always, he held her through the night and promised to face the new dawn with her like she'd always dreamed her life partner would.

11

Kyra could have slept for days. She hadn't realized how poorly she'd been resting at night lately, with too much on her mind. In Ollie's arms, none of that had bothered her. It was like he sheltered her mind the way Van protected her body.

The sun coming through the camper windows hadn't roused her, and neither had Devra's promise of breakfast shouted through the wall—she was still stuffed from the night before—but the unmistakable growl of Van's truck coming up the Hot Rides driveway...well, *that* had her returning to reality fast.

Ollie crawled from bed and tugged on a pair of sweats and a long-sleeved shirt. She was sad to see his tan skin disappearing beneath his clothes, but she figured it wasn't worth him getting frostbite simply so she could admire him some more.

"Van's back." He stood near the doorway, looking through the window over his shoulder, presumably at Van's giant monstrosity of a truck and then at her.

"I heard." She drew in a deep, shaky breath. Like

they'd talked about, there was no taking back what they'd done, not that she'd want to anyway. "I guess we're going to see if he was telling the truth when he said he didn't care if I slept with you. I swear, I won't let him put his hands on you again—I mean, in anger."

Ollie didn't laugh at that. Instead, he frowned. "That's not what I heard him say. I think you've been reading things wrong, and I hope what we did doesn't cause more problems for you. Do you want me to lie? Tell him it never happened?"

"No, of course not." Kyra stood and crossed to him. "I'd never ask you to do that. Aside from the fact that I'm not a fucking liar and neither are you, I think it's pretty obvious."

His hand went instinctively to the hickey she'd given him, making her grin.

"Not only because of that." Kyra avoided eye contact by getting dressed herself. She waited until her face was hidden by her shirt going over her head before she said, "Anyway, it would be good if you don't leave me alone with him right away. Until I can see how mad he is about it."

Kyra held her hand out and Ollie was there, as always, to hold it tight.

"You know he'd never hurt you, right?" he said, without a sliver of doubt in his tone.

"Physically? No. Never." She squeezed his fingers tighter. "But words can hurt too, and so can actions. If he's indifferent or chooses to walk away..."

"I promise," Ollie gave her a tight nod. "I'm not going to let go until you ask me to."

"Thank you." She stood, rising from his bed to greet her other best friend and lover.

Ollie handed her down from the sanctuary of his home and crossed the lawn with her. Van met them in the middle, far enough away from the open garage bays to—hopefully—be out of earshot. When Kyra noticed Walker and Dane popping their heads up and peeking out at the showdown about to happen, she somewhat discreetly shot them the finger with her free hand. Although, it might be for the best to have the duo chaperoning from afar in order to keep anyone from getting another black eye if Van went after Ollie.

The clang of metalworking resumed as they minded their own business, or pretended to.

Like she wasn't going to tell them, Devra and Wren, and the rest of the guys about the outcome of this showdown later anyway. Jeez.

"How did it go?" Kyra asked Van.

"I would ask the same, but I think I already have some idea." He flicked his gaze between her and Ollie, lingering a bit on the dark mark she'd left on his neck.

Ollie fidgeted as if he'd like to rearrange his scarf, but he didn't. Somehow that gave Kyra courage.

"You do." Kyra stood tall and dared Van to go back on his word.

Then she extended her free hand to him and prayed he didn't slap it away.

OPPOSING INSTINCTS WARRED IN VAN. Part of him howled in loss, but another wanted to live up to his promises. He'd had a lot of time alone to do some serious thinking, enough that he'd realized he had really fucked up when it came to Kyra and how he was treating her.

He didn't plan to keep making the same mistakes.

If that meant he had to deal with Ollie too, so be it.

He felt a million times better when he took her outstretched fingers and linked them with his own, which were shivering and not from the cold, either.

It had been pretty clear what he'd find when he returned. He just hadn't known exactly how he'd feel and if Kyra would be willing to give him another chance once she'd realized what a huge crush Ollie had on her too. Hell, Ollie was probably the better bet. He was kind and easygoing. A lot more understanding than Van had been.

"Can we—all three of us—talk somewhere out of the cold?" he asked quietly.

Kyra glanced at Ollie, who nodded. "Yeah, of course," she said.

As one, they turned toward the van, ignoring the Hot Rides office and one of their friends' houses, which might have made more neutral territory. Van knew this was where things were heading, if he got what he thought he wanted.

Ollie gestured for Kyra to go in first. He lifted her knuckles to his lips and kissed them before temporarily allowing her to extract her hand from his. Then he busied himself, turning the driver and passenger seats around on their swivel bases and moving a few things off the bench seat opposite them so they could sit comfortably, facing each other, for whatever came next.

"Cool. I didn't know they did that. It makes this like a living room up front." Van nodded appreciatively. It surprised him when Ollie motioned for him to take what transformed into the driver's seat, assuming he'd have wanted that place for himself.

Was it some kind of message or did he feel better with Kyra sitting between them as some sort of buffer?

Van wasn't sad that she took the passenger seat, next to him. Ollie sat on the bench seat in front of her, completing their slightly skewed triangle. He kicked back, stretching his legs out and resting his folded hands on his abs as if he was completely relaxed instead of tied in knots like Van was at the prospect of the discussion they were about to have. "I'm glad you like it. I was afraid it might be uncomfortable for someone as tall and...big...as you."

"You calling me fat?" Van crossed his arms, but he grinned, trying to remember that he and Ollie had become buddies despite the tension between them and Kyra. They'd spent months hanging out while their mutual friends got to know each other and fell in love.

Van would be lying if he'd said his only fear was losing Kyra. He'd miss Ollie and the camaraderie they'd built if things went sideways now.

"You ought to be given how much you eat, but...nah." Ollie shrugged one shoulder. "I'm just mad I didn't get some of your genes."

Van chuckled, though he stopped when he realized Kyra was staring between them while practically chewing down to the quick what little fingernails she had left after drumming.

"Hey, it's okay." He turned toward her and remembered the mission he'd gone on, the one that should be more important to him than whether or not he ever found his way inside her again. "I checked everything out and I think you're right. There's nothing on the camera footage from that day in the alley or the meet and greets where he's talked to you before. Nothing concerning in the packages he's sent you that are in storage, although there are a heck of a lot of them.

I have to say Number One seems like he's...more socially inept and overzealous than outright dangerous. Guess I can't blame him really. I want to be your number one fan too."

"Oh, thank God." Kyra melted against the seat.

"That doesn't mean I want him close to you, especially when you're alone, but...you were right." As if that wasn't hard enough to admit, Van wasn't finished. He still had the harder part of his revelation to go. "And honestly, the reason I freaked out about it probably had more to do with my own personal feelings about what you did when you were frightened than it did with my professional instincts."

"Understandable." Ollie nodded. "I, for one, am glad you took the incident seriously."

"I bet you are." Van immediately wished he could suck the words back in, but it was too late. They would have to cut him some slack. "Sorry, I'm going to try not to be like that. It's just that I'm jealous as fuck that you were here, sleeping with Kyra, while I was gone."

Kyra turned to him and murmured, "I'm sorry."

"No, you're not." He shook his head, refusing to let her pretend otherwise. "And that's okay. You told me straight up how it was before I left. And I was too stupid to tell you that I wanted to keep you all to myself. I was trying to be mature, let you decide what was best for yourself, and work up the nerve to confess that I don't care if it means giving up my job. I want you more."

"You were?" Kyra tipped her head and narrowed her eyes as if trying to evaluate how sincere he was being. He let her see everything, as he should have for the past several years that he'd been lusting after not only her body, but all of her.

"Yeah. I've been dreaming about having you for the past two years. I just didn't want to ruin what we had or put you in a weird spot because of our positions with Kason's band." He scrubbed his hands over his face, surprised when Ollie reached out and put a hand on his knee for support. "I guess it wasn't until I saw Kason go after Jordan and Wren that I realized how much I was sacrificing by playing it safe. And also that Kason won't hold it against us if we pursue whatever this is between us and, for whatever reason, it doesn't work out."

Kyra's mouth hung open as she stared at him and then Ollie. She said to the other man, "You were right. Holy shit."

Had Ollie been advocating for Van? Why would he do that when he so obviously wanted her for himself? Really, what man who was into women wouldn't go after Kyra? She was bold, badass, alluring, and easy to hang out with. Even when you were dense, like he'd been acting for far too long now.

Maybe both he and Ollie had reached a similar conclusion...Kyra was amazing enough that it'd be worth having any part of her she was willing to give him, even if that meant sharing her with someone else.

"You should listen to me more often," Ollie said with a smirk that cut the tension between them all and set them to laughing.

"I haven't been blameless either." Kyra cleared her throat, then said, "I've been letting my own doubts control my actions. I don't want to be that kind of person anymore. I'm going to be more direct. I intend to say what I mean and mean what I say. Go after the things I desire, even if I don't think I can have them."

"When it involves me, you can have everything," Van promised her. "Even if you want another man too."

"*Madre de Dios*," Ollie whispered under his breath in a perfect Spanish accent, surprising Van.

"*¿Tu hablas español?*" He didn't intend to ask Ollie about speaking Spanish in Spanish, it just came out that way. Probably because he'd been talking to Alanso at Hot Rods most of the times he'd come to Middletown lately.

"*Sí.*" Ollie continued the trend.

Well damn. Van would have to ask him about that later. He always felt more at home speaking in Spanish. Maybe because it reminded him of his mother, his childhood, and all the fun times they'd shared before he figured out that they were poor and on their own in the world. His mother would have adored Kyra, and probably Ollie too, if she were still alive.

Van shook his head, clearing those thoughts before he got too damn depressed.

"Uh, guys... I'm confused enough as it is. In English, please?" Kyra shook her head as she looked between them.

Ollie's mouth tipped up in a wry grin. "Oops, sorry. Although I do like having the option to talk about you without you knowing if needed."

"You would not." Kyra's mouth formed an O that made Van think about plenty of other naughty things he'd like to do with her instead.

Simply to rile her, he held his hand out and Ollie high-fived him. When she slapped their arms down, they cracked up some more.

Yeah, this might not be the worst situation in the world.

"Okay, so..." Kyra settled down first. "Am I cleared to

go back to my usual routine? Are we heading to Kason's place for the rest of the tour break?"

Ollie frowned at that, though he didn't need to.

Van shook his head no. "I don't want you at the mountain house. Even though I didn't find anything too unusual about Number One—the return address on his packages went to a small, tidy home in Des Moines owned by a woman I'm assuming due to their matching last names is his mom—I still take it very seriously that you felt like something was out of place that day. You have good instincts. There's no reason not to implement basic precautions. If this guy is as aware of your schedule and behaviors as it seems, he'll know that's where you typically go on breaks."

"Okay, then what are you suggesting?" Thankfully, Kyra didn't argue.

It uncoiled something within him when she solicited his advice about her security. He didn't intend to abuse her faith either. Van would do what was right for her despite any complications that arose on their personal front because of it. She would always be his top priority. "I think you should stay here with Ollie. And...I think I should, too."

"Good thing I insisted on putting a king-sized bed in here." Ollie whistled.

"Is that okay with you?" Kyra asked him.

"Yeah, of course." He turned to Van then. "But I have one suggestion, if you think it's okay."

"Let's hear it." He wouldn't take any chances with Kyra's safety, but he'd try to accommodate Ollie's demands. After all, he was looking after Kyra too and—okay, fine—she was obviously falling for the other guy.

Van wouldn't shoot himself in the dick by alienating either of them.

"Instead of sitting around here with our thumbs up our asses, waiting for something shitty to happen, why don't we hit the road? I have a few places in mind a day or two drive away I've been wanting to salvage from." He took a deep breath, then said, "I've been to your shows. Now you can see what I do for a change. Not that it's as exciting as being a superstar or anything. Still...it might be fun. Maybe? And it will keep Quinn and Gavyn happy with me. I know they're looking for a few specific things they need to complete holiday projects for clients."

"Road trip!" Kyra whooped. She leapt to her feet and danced. "Yeah. Can we, Van? Would it be okay?"

He couldn't help but laugh at her antics. "Sure. I don't see why not. It's probably better to be away from here, same as from Kason's. People are starting to figure out we hang out here sometimes. In fact, I should probably talk to Quinn and Jordan about setting up additional cameras and a better security system soon."

Ollie spoke up then, giving Van an out he didn't plan to take. "I mean, I know you spend a lot of time on the road in the tour bus. So if you don't want to do it on your vacation, I get that—"

"Nah. It's cool. I get antsy if I have to stay still for too long. And after the years we've spent on the bus, we're used to tight quarters and always being on the move. I'll feel better if we're not at one of our known haunts," Van explained. "If you don't mind extra company, I think your plan is solid."

"Then let's go!" Kyra practically bounced. At least she wasn't pissed Van was crashing the party she'd been having with Ollie. Did that mean she wasn't picking the other guy over him outright? He could only hope.

"I'm going to talk to Kason and Jordan quick. I just want to make sure they're okay with Jordan taking over Kason's personal security for another week or so." Van hoped it wouldn't be a problem.

"I'm pretty sure he'll be doing his best to watch Kason's body regardless. Wren will too, for that matter. I wouldn't fuck with her." Ollie smirked.

"Agreed." Van nodded—she was tougher than most. "I'll be right back. Do you need any provisions for the road?"

He looked at Ollie, who shook his head. "I'm stocked up and ready to pull out as soon as you are."

Van tried not to choke. Either that had sounded dirty as fuck or everything was reminding him of sex now that Kyra was so close. It was going to be a hard ride, literally, the air crackling with anticipation and carnal possibilities. He adjusted his half-stiff cock in his jeans, hoping no one else noticed.

"Hurry up, Van. Take care of whatever you have to so we can get going." Kyra prodded him toward the door. Was it so that she and Ollie could have a few minutes alone, or because she was looking forward to whatever might happen between them on the journey they were about to take together?

He hoped it was that.

Van made his rounds and cleared his schedule for their road trip in record time. As he jogged back to the van, he saw Ollie outside unhooking his power line from the Hot Rides facilities. The guy tucked the cord away, then took one last look around the campervan before meeting Van's stare.

"Get in the van, Van." Ollie cracked up at his own joke, then rounded the hood toward the driver's side.

And that was how he found himself on a road trip, strapped to the middle of the bench seat with Kyra situated between him and Ollie, feeling far less uncomfortable and much more turned on than he'd expected.

12

Ollie sang along to the radio while he drove down some long, dusty country highway. Unlike most times he road-tripped in his van on the way to a junk-heap-turned-goldmine, this time he had both company and accompaniment.

Kyra had grabbed a couple of the paper towel roll cores he kept for Mr. Prickles to play with and was putting on an impromptu drumming performance. While he was blown away by her skill and sheer power, which was obvious even with her primitive imitation of an instrument, Van hardly even cracked a smile. He must be immune to her skillful demonstrations after watching her on stage night after night and undertaking so many miles riding together.

Ollie was not nearly so jaded. He glanced over long enough to admire the strength of Kyra's muscles, which flexed as she nailed the solo, twirling the brown cardboard tubes for extra flair points near the end of the song.

"You're incredible, you know that?" Ollie asked

completely seriously as she came back to reality and tossed her faux drumsticks next to Mr. Prickles cage, behind her seat.

She shrugged. "Just playing around."

Ollie checked the rearview mirror. He caught Van shooting her a wistful glance, though he still didn't utter a single word of praise. Kyra bit her lip, then looked over her shoulder. Van whipped his gaze out the side window to avoid being caught admiring her instead of simply telling her what he thought.

This was going to get old quick. Ollie wasn't the kind of man to tread lightly or hide his feelings. Life was too damn short for that bullshit.

Without thinking, he jerked the wheel hard to the right, sending them careening onto the shoulder as he slammed on the brakes. Mr. Prickles huddled into a ball. When they lurched to a stop, the hedgehog shook himself out then stood up, blinking at Ollie as if to say...

"What the fuck?" Van was on his feet the moment a cloud of dust rose around the now-still campervan. "Did a tire blow?"

Ollie gripped the wheel and stared straight ahead. "No."

"An animal run out in front of us?"

"No."

"Something in the road up ahead?"

"None of that. It's you two. You have to work this shit out. I hate watching you hurt each other, even when you don't mean to." There, he'd said it.

Kyra looked over at Ollie, eyes wide. "Are you insane?"

"Maybe." Ollie shrugged as he unbuckled his seat belt and swiveled his chair so he could face both Kyra and Van simultaneously. Periodically the van shook as a car went past at high speed. "But at least I don't ignore shit and let it fester forever."

"What are you talking about?" Van's eyes narrowed. He cursed beneath his breath in Spanish.

"She's hurting."

"What? Is something wrong?" Van asked Kyra as he knelt by her seat, scanning every inch of her that he could see.

"*You're* hurting her." Ollie stabbed a finger at Van and then Kyra.

Van lost his balance and plopped onto his admittedly tight ass on the van floor. "Me? What did I do? I was just sitting there..."

"Exactly!" Ollie grabbed the guy's shoulder and shook him. "Don't you think she's incredible?"

"Of course I do, asshole," he grumbled as he got to his feet and turned to look at Kyra, who was staring out the window instead of at either of them.

"Then why don't you tell her that?" Ollie shoved past Van and cupped Kyra's cheek. He applied light pressure until she turned to face them. The sheen of tears in her eyes pissed him off and made him want to kiss her simultaneously. How many times had she hidden her pain from Van?

Too many.

No more.

Ollie didn't give a shit if he was about to pay the price for it, he crouched down and leaned in, laying his lips on Kyra's. She sighed and kissed him back, almost as if thanking him for seeing what was right there in front of them. The bad thing was that she flicked her gaze up to Van's, even then seeking his...what?

Approval? Jealousy?

As much as Ollie wanted to help her and Van work things out, he didn't care to be used either. He already had one hell of an attraction to Kyra, and Van had become a good friend. He didn't want to ruin those relationships.

"Here's what we're going to do." Ollie returned to his seat and strapped himself in again. He spun his chair around and said, "Kyra, you good with riding backward?"

"Yeah. I'm so used to spending time on the tour bus, I don't get motion sickness anymore." She watched as he locked himself in place behind the steering wheel again.

"Turn your seat around so you're facing Van. The two of you can talk this through. There's nowhere to run to and nowhere to hide." He cleared his throat. "And if you need a mediator, I'll be here to step in."

Kyra seemed to relax at that. "That would be great. Thank you."

She mimicked his earlier motions and unlocked her seat, freeing it to swivel into the reverse position. When she clicked into place, staring directly at Van, she said, "Hi."

He smiled at that, how could he not when faced with her, and waved. "Hey."

"Okay, here we go." Ollie put on his signal, then carefully checked all his mirrors before merging back onto the highway. So it was a shock when the vehicle coming up behind them in the middle lane swerved over, nearly sideswiping them in the process.

"Holy fucking shit!" Van grabbed at the side door. "How are we supposed to talk when you drive like that?"

"It wasn't me that time!" Ollie shouted. He reached over and tapped the small black box mounted to his windshield, which beeped three times.

"What was that?" Van asked, leaning forward to help Kyra right herself.

"Dash cam. It will save a clip going back ninety seconds." Ollie hated to say it, considering he'd felt like they'd been on the verge of a breakthrough, but he wasn't going to make the same mistakes that they had been. He was going to share everything. "The only thing I saw...or thought I did..."

"What?" Van was on high alert.

"I think the plates were from Iowa." He practically spit the information about his new least favorite state. "Take the memory card out and check the footage on my laptop."

Ollie turned to Kyra next. "Can you use your phone and search for campsites nearby? Maybe we should call it for today."

Van retrieved the camera footage. In security mode, he took charge. "I do think we should lay low, but not on this route. If someone followed us out of Middletown, we need to throw them off. Kyra, look up the next major intersection of highways. Get us at least fifty miles away, then find for a place to stay the night."

"Okay, got it." She tapped and swiped at her phone as Van retrieved Ollie's laptop next. He was silent as he analyzed the footage. Until he roared, "Fuck!"

"I didn't want to be right." Ollie pounded his fist on the steering wheel. "It could be a coincidence, right?"

Kyra didn't say anything. Van grunted. "I'm going to email this clip to Jordan and have him run the plates. Let's make sure."

Ollie nodded, then Kyra told him, "You want exit 227 up ahead. It'll take you to 80W and then you'll have a bunch of options from there. I found places about thirty, forty-five, or a hundred miles away."

Ollie checked the rearview mirror and Van nodded at him. "Hundred."

"Good. Plenty of time for you two to finish your chat." He smirked, trying to remind them of the problems they could control instead of the ones they couldn't as easily.

"I'm not in the mood right now." Van crossed his arms, his expression stormy as he peered at the road up ahead and then checked all around, as if the car that had nearly careened into them was somehow hiding right in their blind spot.

"Will you ever be?" Kyra asked him, surprising Ollie. Usually she didn't challenge Van when he pulled away.

Things were changing. Hopefully for the better.

Ollie concentrated on driving to clear those worries from his mind. They were on this road together. All they could do was keep going.

"I honestly don't understand how you can think I'm the one who's not ready for this." Van shifted some of his foul mood to Kyra.

"Maybe because you told me it was a mistake that one time I kissed you, like a year ago, and then after we fucked, you acted like it never happened." She sounded ten years younger when she asked, "Do you wish it never had?"

"What?" Van rubbed his hands over his close-cropped head. "Of course not! It was the best sex of my life."

"Could have fooled me." She looked at Ollie as if asking him to team up with her against Van.

Unfortunately, he could see both sides from where he was sitting. "Did you seek him out afterward or go back to acting like everything was how it had been before?"

Ollie knew her well enough to know the answer before she confirmed it. "That. I didn't want him to feel weird about what we did. I hoped he'd see it wouldn't make life on the tour bus awkward, or worse, cost him his career."

"I know you meant well, but when you don't encourage him, he feels like he can't tell you what's on his mind because he doesn't realize you'd welcome the way he's thinking about you. He's trying to be respectful and feeling guilty when he's not in the strictest sense of the word." Ollie smiled when Van agreed. "And the reason I know that, is because for a hot minute I was doing that around you too. You might not realize it, but you have an almost instinctual habit of putting guys firmly in the friend zone. That can really screw with your head when you want someone but you also care about not ruining your relationship outside of bed."

"Damn. I didn't know you were so smart." Van drew Kyra's attention back to him. "That's exactly what was happening."

Ollie didn't let him gloat for long. "Then believe me when I say that what you're doing can't continue. She's losing faith in you and your connection. Worse, I think it's damaging her own self-esteem. And I won't let you do that to her anymore."

Kyra grimaced. "Thank you." She put her hand on his thigh and squeezed.

"I'm sorry, Kyra. Honestly. I didn't realize..." Van reached out and took her free hand, enveloping it in his. "You're amazing, beautiful, talented, and my best friend. I thought you knew that. And I swear I won't let another day go by without making sure you understand how much I care for you."

"Kiss me to seal the deal?" Kyra asked, although Ollie knew it cost her.

"Right now? With Ollie here?"

"Never mind." She looked out the window again, refusing to insist.

Ollie slapped his hand on the horn even though there were no other vehicles to honk at. "You two! You're both so damn stubborn."

Van groaned as if he realized what he'd done. They were going right back to their old ways.

Or would have if Ollie wasn't there to short-circuit their dysfunctional patterns.

With a curse beneath his breath, Van unbuckled himself, then leaned forward and slanted his mouth over Kyra's. For a moment, Ollie was in danger of crashing the van—no help from fans without boundaries needed.

He sped up as he recalculated how much time it would take before they could be settled in at their overnight stop. Too long.

Kyra stretched her neck upward, reminding him of how she'd looked when they'd strained together. His cock was instantly hard as he watched Van elicit a similar response. She was so damn sexy it made him ache, and observing Van bring that side of her out turned him on even more.

Did she like to be touched that roughly, or did she prefer his suave style?

Maybe she needed both.

Ollie returned his attention to the road as they broke apart, their uneven breaths evident in the tight quarters of the van.

"In case there was any doubt," Van said, his voice raspier than usual, "I loved kissing you. Just now and the other day and that one time a year ago. I want to do it again. A lot. As soon as we're somewhere sheltered for the night."

"Oh." Kyra smiled, her cheeks pink in the late afternoon sun. "Me too."

Then she turned to Ollie and said, "Drive faster. I want to say thank you for making us do that properly."

It was nearly two hours before they rolled up at the campsite she'd located, booked a spot, and found the place among the long shadows of the rustic facility. The moment Ollie stood and stretched, Kyra was on him, tugging him down for a taste of her lips and the grape lip-gloss she had on.

He wouldn't even mind a few stray sparkles.

Ollie dipped in for one last peck after she separated them, then prepared himself for the bite of the wind picking up outside. He'd need it to settle his cock, which definitely did not approve of that plan.

"Do you still have my gloves?" Ollie asked Kyra.

She looked around and then said, "Oh, I think I stuck them in here so they wouldn't fly around while we were on the road."

Ollie's heart stuttered when she opened the drawer that was empty except for one other thing besides his gloves. His prized possession.

"What's this?" Kyra held up his present.

Ollie took it carefully from her fingers, tucked it back into the drawer it lived in, then shut it firmly. "I'll tell you about it some other time. I'm going to get us hooked up to the electricity main so we can turn on the heat."

"I can think of better ways to warm up," Kyra pouted, though whether about his unwillingness to share with them like she and Van had with each other, or because talking had primed her for something more intense with one or both of them, he wasn't sure.

Van steered Ollie out the door. "Let's go. I'll give you a hand."

He figured that was guy code for *I need to talk to you*, and he couldn't agree more. They had to get their shit together before they spent the night crammed in his bed. Without a plan, who knew what might happen.

Ollie cared too much about Kyra—and, fine, Van too —to destroy what they were trying to build.

13

Van finished staking the awning poles into the ground. Although the cold temperatures meant they likely wouldn't be hanging out underneath the shade structure drinking a few beers while watching the sunset, he figured it would help keep snow from accumulating near the door and the patch of half grass, half dirt from turning into mud that they'd drag inside every time they went up the steps.

The physical labor helped him work off the rest of the energy buzzing through him after his intense discussion with Kyra. It was pretty obvious to him now that they'd needed to hash things out for a while. How much longer would they have kept going in circles if Ollie hadn't broken them from the unhealthy cycle they'd been stuck in?

Too long.

"Thanks for setting that up." Ollie approached from the rear of the van where he'd finished hooking up power and water to the campsite's facilities.

"No problem." Van at least felt useful. It was when he

didn't, like when Kyra had been scared, that he fell into old habits.

He didn't care to go backward. The problem was that the way forward wasn't only up to him. He needed to talk to Ollie before bedtime rolled around. The sun had already sunk behind the line of pine trees across the field. He was running out of time.

"Hey, Ollie?" Van cleared his throat and wondered if his friend would take what he was about to say next as a come on or as the legitimate question it was.

"Yeah?"

"You ever..."

"What?" Ollie wasn't dumb. "Is this about sex?"

Van nodded. "We should probably figure out what our next steps are here and be ready so whatever we need to work out between us doesn't mess with Kyra. What kind of experience do you have with this sort of stuff?"

"I've had a threesome before, if that's what you mean." Ollie shrugged a shoulder as if he hadn't just shocked the fuck out of Van, who'd never done much out of the realm of ordinary. "With two women. I highly recommend it."

Van couldn't help but reflect Ollie's grin as he smacked the guy on the back. "Damn, I never realized how boring I am. I thought I had a great sex life, for the most part—there's never a shortage of eager women around Kason and the band—and now I'm finding out I'm pretty lame. Normal. Vanilla. Whatever you want to call it."

Ollie lost some of his joking nature then. "You can change that, you know. If you want. Nothing wrong with it if you're happy."

"I'm not."

"Yeah, it's killing me too. Being stuck in limbo when it comes to Kyra."

"So you're not into other guys then, are you?" Van wished he'd brought a drink out with him. His throat had suddenly gone dry. Did he hope Ollie said yes or no? It was one thing to imagine both of them pleasing the woman they adored, but what else was he signing up for? Where were they going to draw the line? He had to know before they got naked and things became awkward.

He refused to let weirdness between them to take away from Kyra's enjoyment.

"Shit, yeah. I mean, hasn't everyone kissed their chemistry partner just once to see what it was like or had that wild night where they drank too much and ended up going home with another dude to keep from being lonely?"

Van tried not to stare at Ollie. "Um, no."

"Oops." Ollie shrugged. "I guess I'm not always the pickiest person in the world. If I have a connection with somebody, I'm pretty open to it."

"So you wouldn't be opposed to fucking in front of another guy?" Van tried to play it cool when his heart and his dick were pounding.

Ollie stepped closer. "Hold up. Are you giving the green light for a threesome with you and Kyra?"

"That's what she needs, right?" Van scrubbed his hands over his short-cropped hair. "Is that why she hasn't wanted to sleep with me again?"

"You'd have to ask her to know for sure." Ollie sank onto the van's running board, his shoulders slumped. "But no, I don't think that's the problem. She, um, is pretty... flexible...about stuff like that."

Shit. Van was screwing this up. And now it wasn't only Kyra who was in danger of getting tromped on by his artless ogre-handling of what was obviously a more delicate situation than he'd realized. Thing was, Ollie had taken one look and figured it out.

Van needed him to decipher the puzzle he'd landed them in.

Kason and Jordan had played off each other to win Wren, and the same went for Trevon and Quinn with Devra. Why not him and Ollie for Kyra? Sometimes it took two men to satisfy the right woman.

After the endless days and nights of fun and friendship on the bus, the special day they'd destroyed the bunk, and the emotional exchange in the van earlier, Van was sure Kyra was the right woman for him. He just wasn't sure how to be the right man for her.

"I'm asking you." Van crossed his arms, trying not to unravel further. "Will you help me seduce her and make sure she's so fucking satisfied she can't run away for a week? I figure we'll need at least that long so we can try to figure out what we all want for the future."

Ollie grinned. "I thought you'd never ask."

"So you don't think she'll freak out? My balls have barely recovered from last time she kneed me." Van winced. "I'm holding you in front of me like a human shield if she goes off again."

"You deserved it." Ollie rolled his eyes.

"I know." Van groaned. "That made it hurt twice as fucking bad. I'm trying to do the right thing, but I keep fucking up. I can't keep doing that, not with her and not with you."

"Me?" Ollie whipped his head around.

"Yeah. I'm sorry I screwed things up for you that night and maybe now by having to tag along." Van cleared his throat. "And also for giving you a black eye."

"Apology accepted. Thank you." Ollie held his hand

out, and Van shook it. "For the record, you're not messing things up now. This is what she wants, and maybe this is how it was meant to be all along. There's a reason you two aren't already a couple and why she and I aren't either. Maybe we need each other to really make this work."

"So how are we going to do this?" Van asked.

"Do what?" Kyra wondered as she appeared around the hood of the van carrying her toiletry bag. She'd taken a shower in the unlimited hot water of the campground's facilities and looked even more amazing without her makeup, her hair falling in damp waves around her face.

Ollie looked at Van and gestured wildly. "Just say it."

"We want to fuck you. Together."

Ollie smacked his forehead. "A smidgeon of tact would have been okay."

Kyra dropped her bag in the dirt, utterly forgotten. Had they shocked her? She looked between Ollie and Van, then said, "This isn't some kind of joke, is it?"

Ollie shook his head no and Van confirmed it. "We're not kidding around. We're serious about you. About this."

"What the hell are we doing out here then?" Kyra raced past them and leapt into the van, shedding her clothes as she crossed the short span to the bed.

Van would have told her to stop, so he could do it himself and take his damn time at it too, but when he saw her baring her porcelain skin and the colorful ink decorating it, he was too mesmerized to bark orders. Instead, he followed her lead, toeing off his boots and hopping out of his jeans as Ollie shut the door and put the privacy screens in the windows.

Whether or not he was entirely ready, they were about to find out if this was the best decision he'd ever made or the worst mistake of his life.

14

Kyra shut down the rational part of her brain, which was coming up with all sorts of reasons why they should maybe talk things through or be more responsible and careful with each other before they leapt into bed without looking.

She gave in to the impulsive and greedy parts of herself, which urged her to capitalize on what might be a once-in-a-lifetime opportunity. Her pale pink sweater was over her head and tossed aside before she'd made it two steps inside. As she wriggled out of her pants, she took her phone from her pocket and set it on the countertop, where it buzzed ferociously, vibrating against the hard surface.

Unwilling to be distracted for long, with Ollie and Van in hot pursuit and ready to make her wildest fantasies come true, she barely glanced at it. Just enough to see it wasn't Jordan trying to get in touch with them about the plate he'd been running or the incident they'd caught on the dash cam earlier.

It was probably junk mail since it was from an

unregistered number. She didn't know anyone from the 515 area code. When a picture popped on the screen in the previewer, she shoved the phone away in disgust.

Kyra would let Van deal with that later. Much later.

She sure as hell wasn't about to risk allowing some lame, blurry dick pic to ruin something she'd been dreaming about for months. Unlike the keyboard warrior with no better way to get off than by terrorizing women on in the internet, she was about to have the real thing.

With not one but two men who meant something to her.

So she finished getting naked. After living on a bus of dudes for years, she was pretty skilled in the art of the quick change. Or, in this case, the speedy disrobing.

She'd already laid herself out across Ollie's super comfy bed and struck a pose on her side, her head propped on one hand and the other draped over her hip to hide her bare pussy. Provocative yet not too slutty. At least she hoped.

"Kyra? Are you sure?" Ollie gave her another chance to change her mind, not that she would.

"Huh? I thought that was obvious." She looked down as if only then noticing that she had not a single stitch of clothing on. Colorful tattoos stretched across her chest then wound down her arms. She used her tongue to toy with her lip piercing as she did when she was anxiously awaiting the signal that she was cleared to rush onto the stage.

This was going to be the performance of her lifetime.

If Ollie and Van were going to give this to her, she wanted it to be as good for them as it was for her, and she already knew it was going to threaten to blow the wheels off Ollie's van when they exploded together.

"Yes. Show me that it's not me, it's you. Or at least that it has been until now. I mean, if somebody doesn't take their dick out and put it to good use, I'm going to get a complex." She huffed. "Okay, fine. A *worse* complex."

"What the hell are you rambling about?" Van asked as he got naked, too. Just like that day on the bus, it seemed that once she tripped his libido, there was no going back. Maybe Van needed someone to help him turn off his thoughts every once in a while, too.

Ollie checked the van's doors. Then did the same as she and Van had, hopping on one foot as he peeled off his faded black denim jeans. "I think Kyra very mistakenly believes that we aren't dying to have her."

"What? You're not serious, are you?" Van looked between Ollie and her, his cock halting its progress in stiffening. That was not at all the reaction she was aiming for.

"Don't worry about it. Just...get over here, would you?" She patted the spot beside her. This afternoon they wouldn't be awkwardly attempting to lie in bed without touching each other. No. She would have the decadence of permission. Approval to touch them to her heart's content.

"I'm coming."

"I hope not already," Ollie muttered, making Kyra laugh. It was exactly what she needed to keep from chickening out when faced with the two men she'd been drooling over for months.

"Shut up, asshole." Van swatted at Ollie, missing completely because he didn't bother to turn around or take his stare off of Kyra. "What I meant was staying away from you another moment would be torture."

He leapt onto the bed and straddled her, pressing her flat to the mattress.

"Oh, okay." She hated how small her voice sounded. How uncertain.

"I have an idea," Ollie said as he climbed up behind Van then circled around to her far side and stretched out beside her.

"What's that?" Van asked.

"We shouldn't let her leave this bed until she believes you. Believes *us*." He traced the lines of her tattoos across her collarbones then lower, onto the upper swells of her breasts. His caress seemed twice as potent with Van watching him do it.

"In favor," Van muttered before leaning in until his lips brushed hers when he said, "I hope it takes a *lot* of convincing."

Partially to reassure herself this was really happening, and partially because she'd envisioned it for so long, Kyra stroked her hand down Van's bare back from his shoulder to his tight ass.

If he minded being nude in front of Ollie, she couldn't tell.

Again, it wasn't like there was a lot of privacy on a tour bus. He and the rest of the guys were always strutting around from the shower to their bunks bare-assed. Somehow, though, this was next level.

Van was proud of his body, as he should be given the number of hours he put in at the gym, on daily runs, and with a religious workout schedule he'd designed for the periods they spent on the road.

The funny thing was that Ollie didn't do any of that, as far as she knew, and he too had an incredible physique. One that was leaner and less bulky, but borne of endless hours doing what he loved. Climbing, lifting, hauling, cataloging, and bringing new life to old junk.

They came at things from completely opposite angles and yet ended up so much the same. Was it any wonder she was infatuated with both of them?

Kyra gasped as Van backed away, giving her room to breathe. It wasn't any easier for her, though, when he looked Ollie dead in the face after kissing the shit out of her and said, "Do you get off on that? Watching me make out with her? If not, you should probably say so now."

Fortunately, Ollie appeared to be in the first camp, not the second. His cock was practically poking a hole in her hip, his legs extending down the outside of her thigh while Van's had settled between hers, spreading them to make room for his powerful limbs.

Ollie's voice had gotten awfully hoarse when he responded, "What do you think?"

Van's gaze scanned down Ollie's flushed face, then his torso to his groin.

As if to prove his point, Ollie reached down and fisted his hard-on, pumping it a few times.

"Here, let me do that." Kyra brushed his fingers away and replaced them with her own. He made a handful for her, hot and hard beneath silky smooth skin.

"Damn." He groaned and dropped his head on her shoulder, his teeth nipping at her doing nothing to make Kyra any less turned on by both of the men bracketing her.

"Yeah, you better get him good and hard because after I'm done warming you up, he's going to take you even higher." Van fisted his own cock and tapped it against her pussy. "I'm not a patient man, Kyra."

"Could have fooled me," she grumbled, thinking of all the time they'd wasted dancing around each other.

"Yeah, well, you're tempting me to skip some steps

here and get right to the main event." He teased them both by using the tip of his erection to trace her slit, pausing only to probe at her entrance, reminding her of how damn good he'd felt locked inside her.

"You don't want to wait, either, do you?" Ollie asked in her ear as he monitored her reactions from an inch away.

"No," Kyra reached for Van with one hand and squeezed Ollie's cock with the other. Thankfully he was there to speak for her when she couldn't find the words.

Her body was doing the talking for her.

"Yeah, look at how hard her nipples are, Van. And I bet she's soaking wet already." Ollie tortured all three of them, and goaded Van to do what they wanted, despite any reservations he might be clinging to.

Ollie flicked his fingers over one of her piercings. She tossed her head back as her hips sought Van, pressing up against him and begging him to plunge inside. Then Ollie trailed his hand down the center of her body, between her and Van.

If the back of his knuckles incidentally caressed Van's abs in the process, neither of the guys seemed to mind. As if to test his theory, Ollie slid his palm over her mound, making Kyra moan. He squeezed lightly, the implied possession only making her hotter, especially with Van watching on.

"Yeah. Tell me if she's ready for me. For us," Van barked at Ollie, who did as he was told, his cock twitching in Kyra's hand. Did he like being bossed around?

She hoped so, because it seemed like Van couldn't help himself. It was simply part of who he was to take charge.

Kyra forgot about those technicalities when Ollie's

finger slipped between her lips and rubbed a circle around her opening.

"Oh yeah, she's nice and slick. Her pussy is going to feel so good on your dick." Ollie sighed as his finger sank inside her, testing the resistance of her clenched muscles and massaging her from within.

When she stiffened at the sudden penetration, fireworks already going off in her veins, he held still and let her adjust. Well, he paused the motions of his hand. His lips, on the other hand, kissed a path to her breast, then opened wider so he could suck on her nipple.

"Fuck, yes. She likes that." Van's eyes dilated as he witnessed Ollie toying with her.

Ollie withdrew his hand and lifted his head enough to smirk up at them. "I think she'd like it even better if you fucked her while I take care of the rest."

"Uh huh. Yup. He's smart," Kyra rambled, her eyelids drooping beneath the weight of the lust they were infusing her with. It made her feel sleepy yet extra alive at the same time. "Do that. Please, Van."

He groaned as if he couldn't resist her begging. Maybe he couldn't.

Because just then she felt Ollie retreat as Van advanced. He fit himself to her, so much bigger than Ollie's finger had been, making her aware that she might actually need Ollie to distract her for a few moments as she accommodated Van.

She whispered to Ollie, "Kiss me."

He was there in an instant, devouring her cries of ecstasy and slight discomfort when Van joined them then proceeded to work himself deeper and deeper until she held all of him. Ollie's hand wandered from her breasts to her pussy, his finger rubbing her clit lightly to offset any momentary pain Van unintentionally caused her.

She felt like that might be how things worked between them. Ollie was like the oil that made them into a properly functioning machine instead of one that seized up and ground to a halt due to neglect.

Kyra poured her gratitude and longing into their kiss, sucking on his tongue and basking in the pure admiration in his eyes.

In the background, Van cursed. "You feel so damn good around me. I need more. More of you."

His hands clenched her hips as he began to move, slowly for a few strokes but rapidly escalating to full on fucking.

Ollie pulled away and smiled down at her as she caught her breath. He knew all the right places and ways to touch her to enhance the sensations driven by Van's raw, instinctual movements. Van was powerful while Ollie was dexterous and shockingly precise with his touches.

She held on to his cock, unable to do much but cling to him as sensation overwhelmed her. He rocked his hips, fucking her fist even as Van did the same between her legs.

Kyra was shocked when she felt the first tingles of an approaching orgasm wash over her before they'd hardly gotten started. She never came this fast or without really working for it.

"Ollie..." She tried to get his attention. To warn him.

It was too soon. She didn't want this to be over ever, and certainly not before it had hardly begun.

"Ollie..." she called to him louder this time, more urgently, and his gaze snapped to hers.

"It's okay, Kyra." He brushed hair out of her eyes with

one hand, kissing her cheek as he tended to her. "Don't fight it. Van will love it if you come on his dick. It feels so good when you do that, you know? I can't wait to feel it again myself."

"Good idea. You take a turn," Van commanded. "I need a second to calm down and get my head on straight. If she comes now, I will too. And I don't want this to end yet. That day on the bus...I feel like I reacted instead of being deliberate. I did whatever I wanted without considering her needs."

Ollie glared at Van and knocked his fist into the other guy's shoulder. "That's not going to happen today."

"I know." Van actually looked...embarrassed?

"You have nothing to be ashamed of." Kyra reached up and touched his cheek, her rising desire temporarily suppressed. "Whatever you did, I liked it. A hell of a lot. So apparently we need similar things."

"Same goes for you." Kyra looked up at Ollie, who was tracing her eyebrow with the tip of his index finger. Was he remembering what it had been like to make love as snow fell all around them? She was. She quivered around Van.

"Good to know. So I'm going to kiss you some more while Van makes you come, okay?" He was already leaning in before she nodded.

Kyra parted her lips on a sigh. He was such a good kisser.

The lower half of her body took full advantage of Van's weight and heat between her legs. She rubbed herself against him while Ollie teased her mouth. Having them both—hard and soft, careful and brash, emotional and thoughtful—well, it really was the best of both worlds.

Especially when Van gave her exactly what she needed to get off.

He pumped into her with long, hard strokes that made her feel full and as desired as they claimed she was. That revelation alone was enough to trigger her orgasm, though Ollie's expert manipulation of her clit and the swipes of his lips over hers certainly didn't hurt.

Kyra shouted, her free hand grasping at Van's flank while her other hand clenched involuntarily around Ollie's cock in time to the spasms that began to roll through her.

She exploded, wringing Van's shaft. And she knew he loved it every bit as much as Ollie had promised he would when he stiffened between her legs, grunting and piercing her with short jabs that seated him as deeply as he could get within her.

He called her name over and over as he flooded her with his own release.

Ollie retreated, just enough that his erection slipped from her fingers.

Had he been on the verge of joining them?

She wished he would have. Knowing both of her guys were enjoying this as much as she was would amplify her bliss.

"Damn, that's so fucking sexy. You're gorgeous when you come." Though he aimed his comments at Kyra, she couldn't help but notice that he was watching Van just as hungrily in that moment. The revelation made Kyra clench around Van some more, squeezing his softening cock and some of his seed from her body.

He crashed to her opposite side, breathing as hard as he did when he came in from one of his infamous runs. Knowing she could have that kind of effect on him made her smile and sent aftershocks rippling through her. Even now, she craved more.

Kyra reached for Ollie, nudging him until he climbed over her, taking Van's place.

He lay on her, giving her something to wrap her arms, and legs, around. She nuzzled his neck and sighed when his cock rested full and hard on her mound.

"You want more?" Van asked her, kissing her cheek as he rearranged himself by her side, angling in so he could see what was happening better.

Kyra nodded.

"What are you waiting for, Ollie?" Van asked, his gravelly voice demanding. "Give our girl what she wants."

"Isn't it too soon? Are you sure?" His hard-on told her he craved it, but he held back anyway.

Until Van insisted. "Get in there. I'd do it myself if I could. She needs you."

15

Ollie nodded. He wrapped two fingers around the base of his cock, then angled it so that instead of lying on her, he was poised to penetrate the still-clenching rings of muscle at her entrance.

"He's right," Kyra murmured. "I do need you. Both of you."

On a moan, Ollie slid inside her.

Did he mind that Van had made a mess of her? If he did, he didn't say so. In fact, he seemed even more turned on than he had the last time they'd made love.

His dick felt incredible pressing in, giving her something to hold as her body came back to life around him. As sweet and gentle as he'd always been with her, having Van there or the intensity of sharing her with the other man seemed to ignite a deeper passion in him.

He pistoned within her, faster though more fluid than Van had been.

Despite her epic climax just minutes before, Kyra

knew she was going to repeat the performance before too long if he kept up that pace.

"Yeah, that's it, Ollie." Van didn't give them any space to themselves. He was right there, ordering Ollie to fuck her so well that neither of them would ever forget it. "Deeper. Harder. Make her come all over you. It felt better than anything I've ever experienced before. Her pussy draining my balls dry, just like it's going to do to you soon, too."

Ollie threw his head back, exposing the tendons of his neck to Kyra's hungry lips. She bit him lightly, beneath his jaw, then sucked as he ramped up his thrusts as Van directed.

Van turned to her then and smiled, a shit-eating grin the likes of which she associated more with Ollie than him. Without grim seriousness tugging the corners of his mouth down, he looked even more handsome than she already considered him. Maybe it would be good for the guys to rub off on each other.

"This was a great idea." He crushed his mouth over hers, kissing her with none of Ollie's playfulness or sensuality, but heaps of lust she couldn't deny.

Kyra was starting to believe them. They were into this. And...more importantly...into her.

Her heart soared even as her body ground down on Ollie. Euphoria got her higher than any of the drugs she'd seen people do backstage. She could easily get addicted to the way Van and Ollie made her feel.

Ollie shouted, his cry indecipherable on a verbal level. Still, her body understood his message. He was close. About to join her for another spectacular orgasm.

The first time she'd ever experienced the

overwhelming pleasure of two men attending to her desires.

Though hopefully not the last.

Van lifted his head to look at Ollie. He understood too. "You better make her come with you. Don't shoot until you do or you won't enjoy it as much."

Ollie bit his lip and nodded, focusing on swirling his hips each time their bodies met. The pressure did intense things to Kyra, tapping her clit and encouraging her to meet him stroke for stroke.

"There you go," Van cooed, whether to her or Ollie, she wasn't sure. But the idea of either only enflamed her further. "Just like that. Right there."

Kyra began to shudder, the tension building within her until she couldn't stand it a moment longer. She came, while Van thumbed her nipple piercing and told her over and over how much he loved watching her unravel.

Ollie cried out her name, then Van's, surprising them all.

They seemed to freeze, suspended for a moment, before racing into a frenzy of motion. She bucked beneath Ollie as he pounded into her, finally giving her a glimpse of the man at his core. The one who cloaked himself in jokes and smiles that didn't always reach his eyes.

There was nowhere to hide here.

She'd never felt as exposed or as protected as she did right then. Hopefully it was the same for him. Ollie jerked as he emptied himself inside her then melted on top of her though she was still shuddering and calling his name over and over.

Van noticed her struggling to breathe and rolled Ollie to the side with one hand. It wasn't a shove, but something gentler, more compassionate. Kyra could have sworn she felt herself falling in love with him right then. He cared for everyone around him, but her, and now Ollie, even more than most.

She beamed at Van, who reflected her sense of joy and wonder at what they'd shared. No wonder her friends in this kind of relationship seemed so fucking happy all the time. They had a lot to smile about. Like the fact that although she'd come twice, she could still have more.

"You're hard again," Kyra practically purred as she noticed the stiff cock jutting from between Van's legs. It was every bit as thick and mouthwatering as the rest of him. Kyra reached out and stroked it a few times, loving the heat and hardness in her palm.

"I guess I liked watching the two of you together more than I thought I would." He shrugged, but something flickered over his face as his gaze wandered to Ollie, who was crashed on his side still recovering from his intense climax.

Kyra wondered if it was more than that. Had Van gotten off on ordering the other guy around? What would happen if he let himself top Ollie directly? Would he enjoy that more than orchestrating her pleasure through Ollie, who'd acted as his dirty agent? Would Ollie be open to that too?

That possibility had Kyra eager for Van to take her again. She might be gluttonous, but at least she was honest when she whispered, "I have to have you again."

"Me too." Van crawled closer, kneeing her legs apart before he settled against her core. Ollie reached over and wrapped a hand around her thigh, widening Van's workspace.

He grunted his thanks to Ollie before aligning their

bodies. Kyra arched upward, trying to force him inside her, where he belonged.

He nipped her lower lip, then said, "Let me."

"You like to be the boss, don't you?" Kyra asked him, feeling powerful and naughty at the same time.

"Fuck, yes." He leaned in farther and raked his teeth down her neck. "Don't test me, Kyra. You might not like what you unleash."

She turned her head and looked at Ollie, who was paying rapt attention to their exchange. His eyes were darker than usual, dilated, and not only because they'd drawn the curtains. Despite having just come himself, he was into their exchange, yet separate enough that she knew he'd keep a level head. It was that fact that allowed her to surrender completely to both her own and Van's natures.

If she had any doubt they were on the same wavelength, as always, he snuggled up to her side, kissed her forehead, then murmured, "I'm here. I won't let anything bad happen to you. Take what you want from him."

Kyra's wicked grin slashed across her face as she peeked up at Van, towering over her. "What will you do if I don't obey your rules?"

Whatever he thought of must have been hot, because his cock stiffened enough that when he rocked against her again, he poked the barest bit inside. His and Ollie's mingled fluids made it easier for him to fit this time.

She squeezed down on his cock, antagonizing him with the warm grip of her muscles along his shaft. It felt so good to hold him deep within her that it was a shock to her system when he pulled out in a single fast motion in order to flip her onto her stomach.

He pressed her face into the bedding with one hand as the other lifted her hips until her ass was raised in the air. Ollie took her hand, brushing his thumb over the back of it in soothing arcs. She knew if she clutched it tightly in fear or distress, he'd stop Van in an instant.

So she didn't.

She let it happen, because it was what she had longed for.

"I'll turn this ass bright red if that's what you want. You don't have to fight me to earn a spanking, though I think I owe you one for wandering around by yourself when we're on the road and not telling me right away when you felt threatened." Before Kyra could object, or confess to him about the new text message she was afraid could be from Number One, Van's open hand landed on her ass with a smack that echoed around the interior of Ollie's van.

Heat spread from where their skin had connected. She loved knowing it stung him every bit as much as her. Did it also turn him on?

Because she was wet and eagerly awaiting his return.

Kyra cried out, clearly more from pleasure than pain. So Van spanked her again and again.

Then, when it started to feel like it might be too much, he paused. The heat of his hand was replaced by the blunt tip of his cock tapping against her clit.

She moaned and clawed at the sheets, but no matter how she squirmed, he didn't penetrate her as he kept riding the furrow of her flesh. Teasing her.

Kyra's thighs trembled as she realized he was waiting for her to submit entirely so he could direct their lovemaking. Ollie whispered to her, "Yes, that's right. Let him make it good for you. For us. All you have to do is enjoy what he's giving you."

"Exactly," Van growled.

Ollie rubbed her stinging ass until the burn faded into something deep and desirable.

"Hold her, Ollie," Van commanded. "Keep her still for me so I can fuck her well and make her come apart."

Ollie looked to her for confirmation and she nodded. So he slipped beneath her, taking her arms and placing them behind her, her wrists crossed in the small of her back where he clasped them together and pinned them in place.

Her face was smooshed against his abdomen, as he rested his back against the wall of the van and stretched his legs out on either side of her, flanking Van's knees.

The thought of them touching, even so platonically, as they teamed up to please her, had Kyra frantic to come again. She thought she might encourage them to pick up the pace if she stole some of Ollie's cool rationality. So she angled her face until her lips nuzzled his semi-erect cock.

He groaned. It didn't take much before he stiffened before her.

"You want to suck him?" Van asked.

Kyra hummed, unable to form coherent words any longer.

Van smacked her ass again, then barked, "Do it. Get that cock in your mouth. Do a good job and I'll make sure you fly with him. With me. We're going to do this together."

Kyra had never wanted something so badly in her entire life. So she concentrated on treating Ollie to the best, if somewhat sloppy, blowjob she'd ever given a man in her life.

She opened her mouth and slipped him between her lips however she could, given that she only had her head and neck under her control. It might not have been graceful, but she was enthusiastic as she slid down his length and began to lick and suck his dick.

The fact that she could taste his, Van's, and her own arousal on his skin only heightened her desire.

"Ah, fuck." Ollie grunted as his hips rocked up, feeding her all of him.

"I think I will," Van said, in a tone of voice she'd never heard from him before. It was authoritative and unapologetic.

Kyra's pussy spasmed, coating her flesh in additional lubrication that eased Van's re-entry into her body. Good thing, because he wasn't tentative or gentle. He was fierce as he claimed her this time, bottoming out on the first advance within her.

She cried out around Ollie's cock as Van filled her completely, deeper than ever in this position. His balls tapped her clit as his pelvis impacted her ass, making his glowing handprints there come alive with sensation.

Van put one hand on her hip and began to fuck, his veined shaft stroking sensitive places within her she hadn't known existed before that day. He wrapped his free hand in her hair, using the almost-painful grip to tug her head back.

When Ollie's cock slipped from her mouth, she whimpered and Van froze. "You'd better get it back in there."

Kyra tried but couldn't reach, so Ollie shifted to sit on his heels in front of her while gripping her beneath her arms to help her stay upright.

"You're going to fuck her face, Ollie." Van didn't ask.

Kyra wondered if he shocked himself and Ollie as much as he did her. He was made for this.

Van sprang into action then, when Ollie froze, blinking at the other man as if unsure of what the hell was happening despite how much he obviously liked it. His cock had never seemed so hard before.

"Do it, Ollie," Van coached. "Feed her your cock so we can make her come apart. She's going to unravel between us. Watch."

Kyra wanted to hate that he knew her own body better than she did, but how could she when she was reaping the benefits of his skill and attention to detail?

Van leveraged his hold on her head to maneuver her toward Ollie's cock. She opened her mouth and he did the rest, using her face as a tool to bring his rival ecstasy, although he didn't have to. And that's when she realized that this could be more than a fun way to pass an afternoon while hiding in the middle of nowhere.

This could be so much more than a distraction.

So Kyra applied herself, trying her best to make Ollie pour down her throat while Van went wild behind her. He pumped into her with enough force that his balls kept swinging forward on each pass, giving her clit the stimulation it needed to trip her orgasm.

Or at least it should have been enough. But something in her hesitated.

"Yes. That's right. You're going to wait until I tell you to come, aren't you?" Van's shredded voice got to Kyra. She looked up at Ollie, because he was the key, pleading for him to set off their chain reaction.

He was staring down at her. When their gazes collided, he cursed then shouted her name. "You're so beautiful. So...perfect. I'm going to lose it again."

"Damn straight you are." Van grunted. "Give it to her, everything you have."

Ollie's abs flexed in front of her face. He lurched as if he'd been struck by lightning, then clutched her shoulders as he shot jet after jet down her throat. She attempted to suck him dry as Van began to fuck her harder, faster, but his climax kept going.

It must have inspired Van because he turned frantic, plowing into her hard enough to rock the entire van. He groaned her name, then said, "Now. Come now. With me. With us."

There was no way Kyra could deny him.

Ollie reached beneath her to toy with her nipple piercings as Van's cock embedded as tightly as possible within her. His lunges turned to jabs as he retreated just a bit then locked them together. He released her hip so his hand could snake around and rub irresistible circles around her clit.

Kyra screamed. She flew apart in their arms, held securely between the two men she cared for so deeply. She hugged Van's cock over and over as tremors fluttered her sheath around him. Meanwhile she suckled Ollie's shaft, draining the last bit of release from his balls, using the contact to soothe herself during and after the intensity of her orgasm.

Because it was so beautiful and so blinding that it shattered her completely.

She would have to put herself back together, though she'd never be the same again.

Kyra wondered if Ollie and Van could tell. Or more importantly, if they felt the same.

Because if they walked away from her again now, as if

nothing monumental had passed between them, she might die.

They'd gotten her hooked on them and what they could do to her together.

The high was like nothing she'd ever experienced before. She soared for minutes or maybe more. Kyra had lost all concept of time and anything but the rapture pumping through her veins. She let herself float, absorbing every last bit of joy and pleasure as the guys settled themselves on the bed with her between them.

The soothing caresses, gentle words, and soft kisses they showered her with were a balm that healed so many of the unintentional wounds they'd inflicted on her and she on them. This was what she'd been fighting for. It had been worth it. Would be worth it.

She had to believe that.

16

Ollie shuddered as the kindling they'd arranged caught and whooshed to life with a flash of sinister orange and heat that threatened to sear his eyebrows off. He only put one small bit of wood on top, keeping the flames as low as possible.

"Chilly?" Kyra came up behind him and chaffed his jacket-encased arms. How could she think he was considering what they'd done earlier? He might never be cold again after experiencing...that. *Damn*.

He couldn't think about it now or he'd be standing there with another hard-on.

Unsure of how that was possible when he should be sated for at least a week following not one but the two best orgasms of his life, he tried averting his eyes, except they only landed on Van instead. Ollie shifted, trying to make more room in his pants.

Who wouldn't have been impressed by a primal display like the one Van had put on? It wasn't weird that Ollie was looking at Van with a whole new appreciation, was it?

He jammed his hands in his pockets to keep from doing anything stupid.

As Kyra and Van plopped onto two of the folding chairs he'd dug out of the garage under the bed, accessed from the rear doors of the van, Ollie walked around the fire. It fascinated him as much as it terrified and disgusted him.

While he verified the burn was controlled and contained, he heard the rustle of Kyra opening a bag of marshmallows. Van selected some sticks from the pile nearby. He stripped side branches off them as Ollie returned. "I think these should work. Though I haven't made s'mores since I was little."

"I can't imagine you ever being little." Kyra snorted as she scanned Van appreciatively.

Ollie laughed because, to be honest, neither could he.

"Hey, I have proof." Van fished his phone out of his pocket and tapped a few times before flipping it around to Kyra. "I was a cute kid, no?"

"Aw, super cute." She melted as she looked at the image before handing the phone to Ollie.

Ollie took in the boy with dark brown hair, covered in dirt, and pleased as could be about it. A woman kneeling beside him—with thick, straight hair held back by a navy bandana and warm eyes—was laughing as she wiped a smudge off his face. She reminded Ollie of his mami. "I didn't realize manpris were in style back then."

He took one last look at Van's legs, exposed halfway up his shins by pants he'd clearly outgrown a few seasons earlier, then handed the phone back to him. Hopefully the other guy knew he was only teasing, but he still felt like a dick for the wisecrack. Especially since he figured jealousy over Van's mother was the real reason for his barb.

"Hey, they covered my ass." Van shrugged as if he'd long ago gotten over being made fun of for growing up poor.

That made one of them.

"I personally consider that a crime." Kyra winked at him and slapped Van's butt when he rose from the chair and bent over to put his marshmallow near the flames.

"I would share a baby picture, but I never thought to put one on my phone. I probably should to preserve them, since I only have a couple." Kyra studied her own marshmallow, which she skewered with more force than necessary.

"Why's that?" Van asked, peeking over his shoulder at her before returning his focus to achieving the perfect golden crust.

Kyra sighed then said, "My parents are weird as fuck, you know that."

"I guess. You don't talk much about them, and every time I ask, you change the subject." The fact that Van stared into the fire as he said it made Ollie sure that had stung him.

Kyra offered a shrug that didn't mask her discomfort. "They're some kind of new age hippies, I guess, is the best way to describe it. Believe we're all old spirits living in temporary bodies. So they don't think kids are anything special or that they need much guidance because they should already know how to survive if they look within themselves. I learned to be self-sufficient. Technology isn't really their thing, but at least I grew up with lots of music around so that I found drumming...and my way out. The few pictures I have from back then were mostly taken by friends."

"Well, no worries." Van took his completed marshmallow back to his seat, ruffling Kyra's hair as he passed. "That pic I showed you is the only one I've got. My mom died shortly after that. She and about a dozen other people were riding in the bed of a pickup on the way home from the farm where she picked onions each year. The driver was drunk. He missed a turn and they tumbled down the embankment. They say she died instantly. I hope they're right."

"*Lo siento mucho*, Van." Ollie's heart ached for Van. He knew what it was like to lose the most important person in your universe at such a young age.

"*Gracias*." He sighed as he tucked his phone back into his jacket pocket and sat next to Kyra, carefully assembling his dessert so he wouldn't have to look at them. Kyra's fingers lingered on Van's hand as she passed him a square of chocolate.

Kyra glanced up at Ollie. When he didn't volunteer any information, neither she nor Van pressed him about his own past despite the curiosity he could detect in her stare. Maybe that's what made him comfortable enough to confess. Or maybe it was because he figured it was better to know now if they would shun him once they knew the truth about what he'd done.

Before he grew any closer and more attached to either of them.

Ollie cleared his throat. "You're both doing better than me. I don't have any."

"Baby pictures or family?" Kyra asked, sliding her other hand over to his from her spot between the two men.

Ollie remembered how he'd promised her he wouldn't let go until she asked. He was grateful she was willing to do the same for him. He rubbed the pad of his thumb over her soft skin until the inevitable panic and sickness washed over him as he thought about his mother.

When he opened his eyes, he saw Van staring at the place where Kyra and Ollie were joined. Still, he didn't glare or ask them not to touch for his benefit. If they could go out of their comfort zone for him, he would do the same for them.

"Either." He figured it was easiest to spit it out. "My father had a heart attack when I was five, and a year later my mami..."

Nope, it still got stuck in his throat. The words nearly impossible to say after all this time.

"It's okay, Ollie," Kyra promised. "You don't have to tell us if it's too hard."

He shook his head because...he actually wanted to explain. To remember his mami instead of acting like she'd never existed in order to save himself the pain of her memory. "She died in a fire. That I started."

He didn't clarify because it didn't matter how it had happened. It had been his fault and instead of letting him pay the price for his foolishness, she'd done it instead.

It was fitting punishment that he be left alone when he'd stolen her life. The one person in the world who'd loved him and been there for him.

"Oh shit, Ollie." Van leaned in, resting his elbows on his knees. "I'm sure it was an accident."

"It wasn't." He didn't even have that excuse. "I was stupid. Screwing around with candles in a Christmas decoration. One of those mobiles that turn when the heat rises. I was obsessed with the thing and would play with it constantly, even when my mom told me not to. My father had died so young and unexpectedly, he didn't have life insurance or any savings. So Mami worked as much as she could, cleaning houses, and had to leave me alone for a couple hours here and there. I just, I loved that thing. It was so pretty and mesmerizing to watch the brass angels spin around like magic. And the fire..."

He shuddered again.

Kyra leaned toward him, rubbing his back as he said, "I can't believe I used to like watching the flicker of the flames. Never again."

Ollie swallowed compulsively to keep bile from rising up his throat. "I must have fallen asleep watching the mobile and knocked it onto the floor when I slipped out of my chair at the table. It landed too close to the Christmas tree, which my mom had gotten for free from one of her clients because it dried up and died before the holidays. By the time I woke, the whole thing was engulfed and the fire was licking the ceiling."

"Oh fuck." Van clutched his gut.

"I kept coughing and couldn't think straight. I remember scrambling backward until my shoulders hit the wall. I huddled in the corner and if it wasn't for Mami coming home right then, I would have been the one." Ollie blinked furiously. "It should have been me. Except she broke through the line of firemen telling her she couldn't enter the building and dropped me out the window to them right before the roof collapsed. There was nothing they could do. No hope to rescue her like she'd done for me."

"Ollie..." Kyra made a strangled sound. "She did it because she loved you. I guarantee, if she had to pick between herself or her child, she would have chosen you to survive. And thrive. Even without her."

"That only makes it worse, doesn't it?" He'd told himself the same things in the dead of night when he woke from nightmares, sweaty and desperate to go back in time.

"It was a tragedy, Ollie. Same as the one that took my mother." Van's calm reassurance penetrated Ollie's racing thoughts. "I'm not blaming your mami, she did what she had to, but you shouldn't have been left unsupervised at that age."

"Agreed. Regardless of what my parents believe, kids aren't fully developed creatures inside miniature bodies." Kyra squeezed his hand. "You couldn't have been accountable for what happened when you weren't even mature enough to be responsible for yourself."

Ollie collapsed against the back of his folding chair as if blown over by a gale-force wind.

He'd never thought of it that way before. It didn't immediately erase his guilty conscience, but it did settle the sickness rising inside him enough that he wasn't in danger of losing his dinner after dredging up terrible memories. That was a first.

"Can I ask you one other thing?" Kyra said softly, so he knew it was going to be a doozy.

"Of course." It was too late to hold anything back now.

"That present I found in the drawer, the one that looks like it's been there for a while..." She knuckled moisture from her eyes. Was it from the cold or the smoke from the fire or was he upsetting her with his story?

"It has. The fire happened two weeks before Christmas. Mami had it wrapped and hidden in the glove compartment of her car. The caseworker went through the vehicle looking for any information on next of kin, though there wasn't any since my mother had moved here from Mexico with my father. She gave it to me before I went into the system." He knew what Kyra would ask next, so he gave her the only answer he knew for why he hadn't opened the damn thing. "I guess it felt like if I kept it, she would always be there in some way. If I unwrapped it, then it would just be me. No more presents from my mami. Ever. Besides, I didn't deserve a gift considering it's my fault she never got to celebrate another holiday."

"It's not!" Kyra stood then and rushed to Ollie, flinging her arms around him. "Please stop saying that. Your mami wouldn't want you to take that on yourself."

Her tears streaked down his neck where she buried her face against his skin.

"Sometimes horrific things happen in life. It doesn't have to be anyone's fault." Van approached too, putting one hand on Kyra's back and the other on Ollie's.

"I know that. And what you've said helps some. But I still can't stop wishing it had been me and not her who suffered the consequences when I refused to listen to her warnings." Ollie clutched Kyra then, afraid that if he let her go he might shatter. He'd never said those words out loud, but they'd been eating away at him for two decades. "She told me what could happen and I didn't listen. I didn't really understand until it was too late."

"I'm so sorry," Kyra murmured in his ear before kissing his cheeks over and over, rocking him until he could find the air to take a deep breath again.

And when he did, he figured he might as well go all the way and admit some more ways in which he was fucked up. That night had razed him, too.

"Here's the thing, Kyra...I realize that sometimes you

think Van is overprotective and stifling." Ollie still clutched her, so he felt it when she nodded against him. "But honestly, that makes me feel better. I haven't been able to let myself feel for someone the way I feel for you. I tried—so damn hard—to keep myself from falling for you, too. Especially since there are times where you're going to be far away from me, where anything could happen and I won't be there to stop it. After getting to know Van, and seeing how he takes care of you, it clicked. He does a far better job than I could ever do to protect you. That's what made me comfortable enough to move forward. *That's* why I caved and kissed you after the concert that night. I'm glad you have him looking out for you. One reason I think I've never been open to a long-term relationship before was because..."

"You're afraid of losing someone you love," Van said simply.

"Yeah." It was true even if that made him a coward.

"I get that." Van paced in front of them. "After we buried my mom, I didn't know what to do. I got schlepped around with all the other kids of the migrant workers until I was fifteen, and I ran away, looking for...I don't know what. I ended up in New York, walking around the city all night, until the dizzying lights made me realize I was truly on my own. I had no idea what to do with the rest of my life. Some assholes tried to jump me and I fought back. The guy who owned the bar next door saw. Carlos took me in, cleaned me up, and offered me a job as a bouncer. Even then, I was big for my age. He never asked how old I was and I never told him. Besides, it was my job to take people's keys and call them a cab when they'd had too much to drink, which felt right, considering... Anyway, after a couple of years saving my money, I started taking riskier jobs that paid better until I had my own security service. I don't know if I was meant to do this, or if it's some kind of crutch that helps me get by because of what I've been through. But I do believe there's a purpose for all of us, and I'm glad that my twisted need to do this somehow made your fucked up brain rest a little easier."

Ollie never would have thought it was possible, but in the middle of everything, Van made him laugh.

On that note, they sat in silence for a while, each of them lost in their own thoughts about how they'd gotten there, how they fit so well together, and what they should do about it. Ollie finally allowed his panic to retreat enough to admit to himself that he was already in love with Kyra. And Van...well, the guy was becoming something like a best friend. Except more...

Someone he wouldn't mind being bound to forever by the woman they both adored.

The fire had died down to embers by the time Ollie realized Kyra was hugging herself to stay warm. Neither she nor Van had stacked more wood on the blaze after his disclosure, and soon it would put itself out. The moon and stars were barely enough to see by and, in the distance, coyotes howled.

"We should probably go in," Van said.

As much as some part of Ollie urged him to take refuge in his home and pretend they'd never had this conversation, he couldn't. Not yet. "Go ahead. I'll be inside in a few minutes. As soon as I make sure this fire is really out."

He stood and took the hose he'd laid out before lighting the bonfire, preparing to douse everything inside the circle of stones and what lay a few feet beyond it for good measure. He'd never risk Kyra's or Van's or Mr.

Prickles' or anyone else's safety. Not even his own. Never again.

"I can do that for you," Van offered.

"Nah. No offense, but I won't be able to sleep if I don't see it for myself." Ollie wondered if anyone had ever noticed he was always the one to put out the fires they sat around at Hot Rides. Those summer evenings had been some of his best nights, and also a vivid reminder of why he didn't deserve to be as happy as the rest of them.

"Okay. I get that." Van put his hand on Ollie's shoulder and squeezed. "I would do the same if I was you. I'll hang out until you're comfortable, give it a double check if you'd like."

"Yeah, that would be great. Thanks." Out of the corner of his eye, Ollie spied Kyra watching them.

She smiled, blew them a kiss, then headed inside saying, "I'll feed Mr. Prickles and start some hot chocolate."

"I can think of better ways to stay warm tonight." Van bumped his shoulder into Ollie, knocking him slightly off balance. His hand reached out and steadied Ollie. If it lingered a little longer than necessary in the middle of his back, neither of them mentioned it.

Ollie murmured, "Sounds good to me."

17

"**K**ason didn't say why he needed you back right away?" Ollie asked for what had to be the tenth time since they'd gotten the call and turned around.

"No, but let's be honest." Van rubbed his hand over his short-cropped hair. "I didn't like being out there, so alone and exposed, after what happened yesterday anyway. We came on this trip to escape attention but it seems like maybe it was too late for that."

Kyra squirmed in her seat. Was she uncomfortable given how well they'd used her the day before and again that morning before hitting the road? Or...maybe she'd had too much coffee.

"Do you need me to pull over at a rest area?" he checked with her. "Or if you're brave you can use my bathroom while I'm driving."

"I am an expert at taking care of business while underway," she shook her head. "It's not that. I, uh, have to tell you guys about—"

Whatever she'd been about to say got drowned out by

Van's phone ringing. He muttered in Spanish low enough that Ollie didn't quite catch what he said other than a distinct curse. Then he connected the call and put whoever it was on speakerphone. "Is there something you're not telling us, Kason? What's the big fucking hurry?"

"Calm down, big guy." Kason laughed. "Nothing's wrong, I swear. We're just...excited for you to get here, that's all. Maybe I miss you."

"Yeah, right," Van grunted. "I've only been gone for a fucking day and a half, which you probably spent in bed with your girlfriend and boyfriend."

"Actually, nope. We were busy." Kason sounded smug.

"Doing what?" Van wondered.

"You'll see. How far out are you now?" Kason wondered.

Ollie checked the GPS, then said, "Less than an hour."

"Great! See you guys then." Kason chirped. Before they could pry any additional information out of him, he hung up. Van glared at the disconnected phone in his hand.

"Well, it definitely didn't sound like he's having a crisis." Kyra shrugged. They would know since Van and Kyra had been instrumental in pulling Kason out of a spiral of depression and addiction a few years earlier.

They spent the next forty minutes debating what they would find when they rolled up the long, winding driveway to Kason's luxurious mountain retreat near Middletown, home of the Hot Rods and Hot Rides sister-shops.

Ollie certainly hadn't expected the expansive stone parking area to be full. Classic cars, beautifully restored, took up most of the space and a line of equally sexy motorcycles occupied the other side. He parked his campervan directly in the middle, wondering if he was in for another lecture about how their friends could spruce up his home inside and out.

Mustang Sally had been begging him to let her design a custom paint job for months. Maybe he should cave and let her do her thing. He just hadn't decided exactly what he would like other than the boring factory silver with his company's name in stick-on red vinyl letters, which rounded out the campervan's current exterior finishing.

"Looks like they started the party without us," Kyra said as she unbuckled and slid out of the van.

Although Ollie expected Kason to greet Van and Kyra, who were his best friends, the man was nowhere in sight. He noticed the stare the two exchanged. Though they weren't the jealous sort, it probably took some getting used to now that Wren and Jordan were Kason's priorities.

Ollie figured he'd do his best to fill that void.

He knitted Kyra's fingers in his and put his hand on Van's shoulder, pushing them up the grand stairs to the wood and glass mansion, perched on top of a mountain, overlooking picturesque Lake Logan.

Before they'd reached the front door, it opened and Trevon welcomed them inside.

"Hey, you made it!" He shouted over his shoulder, "Someone go tell Wren that everyone on her list is here!"

"What exactly are we late to?" Ollie wondered. "And should I be more dressed up? I don't really have fancy clothes, but I could probably find something a little nicer than this..."

He gestured to his standard long-sleeved shirt and jeans. They kept him from getting too scratched up on salvage runs but weren't especially fashionable.

"Nah. They told us to come as we are." Trevon shrugged. "To be honest I have no idea what's up their sleeves. But they said something about an early holiday party and paid Devra to make a shit ton of food. Hell, even the Powertools crew came over."

Trevon finished his explanation as they reached a few of the other guests milling around.

"My bet is Wren's knocked up," Dane said with a grin. "Based on the number of times I've walked in on her, Jordan, and Kason going at it in the back room or heard it from over at Quinn's place, I'm thinking I've got good odds."

"A baby?" Kyra squeezed Ollie's hand. "Really? That would be amazing!"

Walker shot his partner a glare and slapped him in the back of the head. "You can't just say shit like that. Someone who doesn't know better might think you know what you're talking about. Especially about something so important. A kid isn't a joke, asshole."

Dane flipped Walker off, then went to grab a refill on his plate of appetizers.

"Sorry about that." Walker shook his head. "He's a dumbass. Please don't listen to him."

"Well, whatever it is must be important since they went to all this trouble." Van scanned the room and Ollie knew he was verifying everything was secure. Members of his team were positioned near several of the doors and they'd had extra guards stationed at the gatehouse.

Jordan wasn't taking any chances with the safety of his lovers or their friends.

"Maybe I should go check with my team..." Van started to take a step toward them when Kason appeared at the railing.

Ollie still couldn't get over how fancy his place was. Overlooking the great room, the balcony was only two thirds as tall as the mammoth pine tree, sparkling in front of the three-story glass windows. On the far wall a floor to ceiling stone strip encapsulated a gorgeous fireplace, complete with a snapping and crackling fire.

He skipped quickly past that, trying not to think about how the entire place was made of timbers or how near the flames were to the Christmas tree. Kyra held his hand tighter, her grip reassuring.

A few older kids he recognized as Mike's and Joe's from the Powertools crew played with Nola and Kaige's daughter, and a couple of the other mini Hot Rods. It was hard keeping track of them all. The rest of the local gang, their friends from out of state, plus Tom and Ms. Brown, collectively gave their attention to Kason.

He had a way of capturing people's focus. Ollie guessed that was what made him a star.

Kason projected so everyone could hear him even without his usual microphone. "Good evening, everyone. Thank you for coming!"

"Not that I don't enjoy a good party, but...what are we here for?" Tom asked what everyone was thinking. As the honorary patriarch of their group, he spoke for them all.

"To celebrate my wedding." Kason had never smiled as wide as he did when he shocked the crowd. "I asked Jordan and Wren to marry me and they both said yes. We don't want to wait. So...let's do this."

"Shit, I *am* underdressed." Ollie looked at his scuffed boots and grimaced.

"If you are, everyone is," Kyra pointed out. "Even Kason is wearing jeans."

Okay, that was a fair point. Besides, he knew Wren

wasn't the sort of woman to stand on tradition. It did surprise him when she emerged behind Kason, wearing a sexy red satin dress. Jordan was with her and, not so different from how Ollie had come inside with Kyra and Van, he clasped one of Wren's hands and one of Kason's before leading them both down the sweeping circular staircase.

Their friends swarmed them, offering congratulations as they made their way to the base of the Christmas tree, where they stood in a triangle and everyone crowded around.

Wren smoothed down her dress, still nervous about having on something other than her welding gear in public, he was sure. Though she shouldn't have been because she looked incredible.

She said to Devra as they hugged, "I thought I'd carry on your tradition and wear red."

"I approve." The woman swiped a happy tear from the corner of her eye as Quinn and Trevon looked on, shaking hands with Kason and Jordan while they offered their congratulations.

Ollie smiled as he thought back on the time he'd tried to flirt with Wren and had imagined she might be someone he could love, before Kyra—and Van—had crash-landed in his life. What he'd felt for Wren had been intense, more powerful than anything he'd experienced before. Still it paled when compared to how he felt about the woman, and her lover, who now shared his bed.

Wren had known what he hadn't—they were meant for other people.

When she looked his way, he grinned and nodded. "So happy for you."

Kyra wasn't having any of that. She charged across the

gap between them and flung her arms around Kason. Van piled on. Ollie knew they'd seen the man through some rough times. This was a victory for them too.

He edged closer, wanting to be near them and share in their joy.

Jordan didn't miss it either. He raised his brows at Ollie, then said quietly, "Maybe it'll be your turn next."

"Uh, I doubt it." He wasn't sure what else to say. Though he'd dreamed about their fling lasting, it was still far too fragile to declare his desires so openly.

Except Kyra chose right then to turn toward him. She frowned at his response.

Shit.

He knew she battled her own insecurities about being desired, and now that he had more information about her upbringing, he could see why that might be an especially sensitive spot for her. Before he could clarify, they were being swept aside by more of their friends edging in to give their well wishes to the established trio, who were declaring their relationship official and permanent that night.

Ollie stood by Kyra and Van, watching as Kason, Jordan, and Wren exchanged simple promises, though ones that counted for so much. They slid matching gold bands on each other's fingers and sealed their vows with a threeway kiss that made Ollie's mouth go dry.

Though he tried desperately not to glance over at Van, he did anyway. A shock of awareness jolted him when he saw the other man staring back, equally as intent.

Kyra glanced up and caught whatever it was passing between them. She smiled and leaned her shoulders against them, forcing them to step closer to keep her upright.

Together, they held her as their friends promised each other forever.

And when the impromptu ceremony was over and people had dispersed throughout the massive house to eat, drink, laugh, and dance to Kason singing "The Real Thing" for his new wife and husband, Ollie excused himself from Kyra and Van, then went off in search of his boss.

If he wanted to try for that kind of happiness in his life, he was going to have to make some major changes.

Fortunately he stumbled across Quinn, the Hot Rides shop manager, chatting with Gavyn. They were nestled into a sitting nook away from the majority of the merrymaking. He came up from behind them and swung around the end of the enormous leather sofa they were lounging on.

"Hey, Quinn, Gavyn, can I talk to you guys for a second?" Ollie leaned against a nearby case that displayed at least a dozen awards Kason had won for his music.

Which was when he noticed Amber sitting on her husband's lap, surrounded by Gavyn's thick arms. Her head rested on his shoulder as if she could barely stay awake.

"Oh, sorry. Didn't realize this was a family meeting. I'll catch you another time, when we're back at Hot Rides." He turned to leave them in peace.

"Ollie, wait." He glanced over his shoulder at Amber, who got to her feet more gingerly than usual with one hand pressed to her baby bump. She was really starting to show now, six or seven months into her pregnancy, he guessed.

Rather than make her come to him for whatever it was she wanted, he crossed to her, saving her the trouble. She wrapped him in a warm and surprisingly tight hug.

"What's that for?" he asked, peering over her shoulder at her husband and Quinn, both of whom were smiling softly instead of looking like they would rip his head off for touching her.

"I'm hoping someday you'll realize that you're part of our family now." Tall and athletic, she didn't need to go up on her tiptoes to kiss his cheek. "Now I'm going upstairs to commandeer one of those ridiculously comfortable-looking bedrooms to take a nap. Come get me whenever you're ready to go home, Gavyn. No rush. I'll get out of your way so you boys can discuss...whatever it was you had in mind."

"Sure you don't want me to tuck you in?" Gavyn asked, a hopeful note in his tone.

"If you do, neither of us will get any rest, and I'm not sure we know Kason quite that well yet." Amber chuckled as she wandered toward the stairs, stopping to talk to a few of their friends on her way.

Gavyn slumped on the couch before shooting Ollie and Quinn a lopsided grin. "If she wasn't so damn exhausted after helping Wren and Devra organize everything tonight, I would have done it anyway. It's a good thing you're going to take over running Hot Rides for me, Quinn. Once the baby comes, she's going to need my help to keep her event planning business strong."

"Are you looking forward to being a stay-at-home dad?" Quinn asked.

Ollie listened intently as he sank onto a chair facing the two men, who'd known each other for years.

"Yeah. You know how it is, Quinn. Family first. Amber is everything to me and soon there's going to be a new person who's part her and part me. How can that not be the most amazing thing in the universe? I can't wait to meet our child." Gavyn seemed utterly content. "You'll see someday, I'm sure. Assuming that's what you, Devra, and Trevon want."

"She talks about having kids, yeah." Quinn drew in a deep breath then blew it out. "I'm just not sure what kind of father I would make. I mean, I don't even know who mine is and...well...we all know my mom wasn't Parent of the Year material."

"Shut the fuck up. You would be a fantastic dad." Ollie blurted it before he thought too much about the fact that Quinn was his boss and he was here to ask a favor. Probably not the wisest way to speak to the guy. But they were friends too, and maybe Amber had it right...maybe they were starting to be his family.

Fortunately, Quinn only laughed.

It was Gavyn who didn't. "Quinn, that's some serious bullshit. You're already the natural leader of the Hot Rides and take care of everyone at the garage. You're nothing like your mother. Did she ever have a lasting, loving relationship?"

Quinn shook his head.

"You do." Ollie pointed to where Trevon and Devra were mingling with Sally, Alanso, and Eli from Hot Rods and James, Neil, and Devon from the Powertools crew. Every few seconds, one or both would glance over at Quinn as if making sure he was real. They were smitten, both of them.

"Still kind of in shock about that." Quinn shook his head slowly. "But glad and so damn grateful. Same with the shop stuff. Thanks for trusting me, Gavyn."

"You earned it, kid," Gavyn said. "So why don't you see what Ollie wants?"

"What *do* you want, Ollie?" Quinn grinned. "I'm in a pretty good mood at the moment, so it's a good time to ask for a raise or whatever."

Ollie choked. "Nothing like that. I mean, you already pay me *very* well."

"You're worth it." Quinn seemed dead serious.

"Okay, so hopefully you can work with me on this." Ollie drew a deep breath then made his proposal. "I want to stick close to the tour bus when Kason, Kyra, and Van are on tour."

"I fucking bet you do." Gavyn smothered a chortle behind his hand. "You weren't even gone for two whole days. Sounds like it was a productive outing, though."

Ollie couldn't help but grin in return. It had pretty much been the single greatest time of his life. "Yup. So, I was thinking maybe Kyra and Van could stay with me and when they're prepping for shows, I could salvage places nearby. Since they travel the entire country, I could hit up places I don't normally go and haven't already rummaged through."

"Let me get this straight..." Quinn deadpanned, making Ollie nervous as hell. "You want to ride around with Kyra and Van in your van?"

Gavyn howled with laughter, doubling over and clutching his gut. "Van in his van. Oh God, how didn't we see that coming? Van in his van!"

Ollie smacked his palm against his forehead. Screw it, he laughed too. "Um, yep. Except I'd much rather be riding Kyra in the van, if you know what I mean."

"I do." Quinn slapped Ollie's knee. "Hell yeah, that's a

great idea. Of course you should do that. And don't come back until you've joined the club."

"Which club would that be?" Ollie wondered if Quinn was referring to the fact that he and Trevon as well as Kason and Jordan were lovers in addition to sharing their women. It might not be the worst idea ever...

He instinctively sought out Van across the great room, their gazes colliding before he jerked his away and refocused on Quinn and Gavyn.

"The Happily Ever After Club, of course." Gavyn looked at Ollie like he was dense.

"Ah, yeah. I don't know if I can pull that off. But...I'd like to try, at least." His stomach flip-flopped as he thought about how high the stakes were getting and how fast. Everything about it felt practically fated, though, so he plowed ahead. "I think they're the perfect people for me. I just don't know what I am to them. Maybe I'm a novelty. Maybe Van will get tired of sharing his woman with me."

"Don't let Kyra hear you say dumb shit like that." Quinn shook his head. "She's no one's. Maybe she'll be good enough to share Van with you."

"Well, I don't know anything about that." Gavyn shrugged. "But you all seem happy tonight, more than I've seen you before, so that's a great start."

"Hey, don't knock it 'til you've tried it," Quinn teased his friend.

"Pretty sure Amber would slice my dick off if I did. I mean, at least if I didn't invite her too." They all laughed at that. Mostly because it was true.

"What's so damn funny over here?" Van asked as he approached with Kyra.

Ollie gulped, wondering how much the guys would divulge.

"The fact that it looks like you three are going to have to learn to squeeze into one bed on the road." Quinn didn't betray the most sensitive details of their discussion.

"We are?" Kyra asked, her voice definitely excited and not full of dismay.

"Would you like to try it?" Ollie asked her and Van. "Quinn says it's okay if I follow along with the tour and salvage as we go. So if you want...you could stay with me. Both of you."

"Wow. That's...great!" Van picked Kyra up and spun her around. "A huge upgrade from separate bunks and zero privacy on the bus."

None of them said it, but Ollie was pretty sure all three of them were thinking it. *And liberty to get it on whenever we want.*

"Seriously, Ollie. I would love that." Kyra leaned down and kissed him, right there in front of their friends and anyone else who cared to look. Then she did the same to Van.

Quinn and Gavyn bumped fists like they had a plan and it was coming to pass exactly as they'd intended. Ollie eyed them suspiciously, but he was too damned ecstatic to care if they'd somehow played him.

"Guys, if you'll excuse us. I think there's something we have to do." Ollie didn't care if everyone knew that *something* equaled fucking. He needed Kyra, and to be closer to Van through their mutual enjoyment of her. Right then. He couldn't wait for the reception to die down. With this crowd, it was likely to continue for the entire weekend anyway.

"Yeah, each other." Quinn snorted. "Have fun. Be safe."

Ollie nearly tripped at that. It occurred to him that they hadn't been. Safe, that was. Neither he nor Van had worn a condom the day before and he'd been distracted enough that he hadn't questioned it.

He grabbed one of Kyra's hands and one of Van's, in what was becoming his signature move, then practically dragged them outside. When they were alone, he said, "Um, it's kind of late to be having this talk now, but..."

His concern must have been evident in his expression.

"It's fine, Ollie. I'm on birth control. Other than Van, I haven't been with anyone in pretty much forever." Kyra groaned. "So can we please go make up for that right now?"

"Hell, yes." Van picked her up and tossed her over his shoulder, making both Kyra and Ollie laugh. He strode toward the campervan with a shout over his shoulder. "Keep up, Ollie. I'm not going to be able to wait."

And he didn't.

The sex was fast and furious and even more satisfying than the first time they'd experimented with a threesome. He wasn't sure how their lovemaking could improve, but he couldn't wait to see what it might be like the next time and the time after that as they continued to discover how to delight each other and shed their inhibitions together.

A long, long time later, Ollie flopped onto his back in bed between Kyra and Van. From that position he was only a few feet away from his mami's gift, tucked safely in its drawer. He couldn't say exactly what it was that made him think of it—maybe being with two people who had inspired him to love again, and witnessing Wren, Jordan, and Kason's pledges earlier, had him overly sentimental—but once he did, he couldn't shut it down.

"Guys..." Ollie cleared his throat.

"Yeah?" Kyra shifted and settled her head on his shoulder.

"What's up?" Van asked.

"I know it's a bit before Christmas, but...I was thinking...maybe it's time." He didn't have to elaborate. They knew exactly what he meant. Of course they did.

"You've waited long enough." Kyra patted his chest.

"Go ahead." Van nodded. "I'm sure your mami wouldn't mind."

Ollie's hand shook as he reached over Kyra and opened the drawer. He took the present from inside and turned it over and over in his hands, like he had often in the past, on days that he was struggling. Whatever it was didn't weigh much and wasn't very big either.

"You deserve everything good people choose to give you," Kyra murmured in his ear before kissing his cheek.

"She's right. You're a decent human being, Ollie. I'm very fortunate to call you my...friend." Van stumbled over that last bit, but Ollie believed him when he said it.

So he slipped his finger beneath one of the folds and put light pressure against the tape that had held it down for the past twenty years. "I don't know if I can do this."

Did Kyra and Van realize this was about so much more than a gift?

"You owe it to yourself to try." Kyra put her hand on his knee and squeezed. "And to your mami. Because she wouldn't have wanted you to live half a life, closed off, alone and afraid. It's disrespectful if you don't make the most of the opportunity she gave you."

Oh, yep. They got it. Got him. Completely.

And that gave him the courage to push harder.

The paper ripped.

Ollie felt as if he was exposing his heart and soul—instead of whatever had been safely ensconced in the festive, if faded, wrapping—to the world. Once one tiny corner was revealed, the rest got easier. He popped the tape on the other side. Then he couldn't stop. He tore the present open, sitting up so he could see what tumbled out into his shaking hand.

Kyra and Van hovered over him, utterly silent.

A chocolate-brown leather cord was wound around a rectangle, not much bigger than a postage stamp. He unwrapped it loop by loop, holding his breath.

And when he got to the center, he realized exactly how precious the thing he was holding was. Because right there in his palm, was his mami, smiling up at him, even more beautiful than he remembered.

"I was so scared I'd forgotten what she looked like or the sound of her voice. But I look at this and she's exactly like I see her in my dreams." Though prepared to be embarrassed with full on man tears, Ollie was surprised to realize that the image didn't hurt. He smiled, joy and light blasting through every cell of his body, as he recalled all the times they'd spent together. They might not have had a lot of stuff, but they'd had each other. "She taught me how to smile, and to enjoy life, even when it didn't go how you planned. Especially when you lived through loss. She kept laughing, always."

"So have you." Kyra, however, was doing the crying for him, it seemed. Tears poured down her cheeks as she watched him stroke the photograph with his index finger.

"And you were a pretty cute kid too," Van said, his voice more gruff than Ollie had ever heard it, even when he was buried inside Kyra and about to erupt. No digs about his faded shirt with mismatched buttons or his slightly uneven haircut, courtesy of his mom.

The picture sparked a memory he'd lost before this. One he would treasure as much as the rustic locket his mother had obviously made herself. Of her, sitting him on the kitchen counter and snipping away at his hair.

"Do you miss Papi?" he'd asked her.

"Of course, son." She smiled despite her pain. "But the worst thing we could do would be to forget and to spend our whole lives crying, when he'd be so much happier to hear us laugh."

Then she'd tickled him until he'd gone hysterical with it despite the fact that his hair had remained spiky on one side.

"You guys, and the Hot Rides, and everyone else who keeps telling me shit I don't listen to are right." Ollie put the leather cord around his neck and covered the photo with his hand, trapping it close to his heart. He refused to dishonor his mother's spirit by letting his fear of losing things keep him from living his best life.

Which was good, because right then he needed to be extra bold and extra brave.

Ollie took an enormous breath, and stared into Kyra's eyes. He said simply, "I love you."

"I love you too, Ollie." She kissed him then, with so much tenderness that he knew it had been the exact right thing to do. And when they broke apart, grinning at each other, he realized Van had retreated a foot or two away.

Ollie nudged Kyra, who glanced over at her other lover, held out her hand to draw him near again, and said, "I love you too, Van."

"I love you," he promised Kyra before crushing her, and Ollie with her, in one hell of a hug.

Ollie spoke straight from his heart. "Whatever happens after tonight, I want you two to know that this has been the best day of my life and I hope to keep breaking that record with you both, often."

As if he agreed, Mr. Prickles chose right then to bite the bars of his cage, rattling them until the three of them looked over at Ollie's pet.

"Yep, I think that's a terrific plan, too, Mr. Prickles," Kyra told the hedgehog before sticking her fingers into the cage to pet him. The animal leaned into her gentle caresses. Ollie could relate.

When the three of them finally curled up together under his fluffy duvet, he slept more soundly than he had since before the fire that had nearly burned his life to the ground.

18

"This is the life," Kyra purred as she stretched out between Van and Ollie. "We have our own space. Privacy. No noisy-ass bandmates up late hanging out or a race for the shower in the morning. I could really get used to this."

Van grinned. "I'm already used to it. Sorry, Ollie. Looks like you're stuck with us."

"I do not mind one single bit." Ollie rolled over, the now-familiar glint in his eyes proclaiming that his morning wood was about to be put to good use.

It had been two weeks on the road together since Kason and the band had gone back on tour. They only had one more show, tonight, and then they'd be off for the holidays. The reality was, Van felt like he was already on vacation. His whole life seemed like one incredible trip, because he spent it with Kyra, the woman he loved. And Ollie...

Whatever he was becoming. Best friend? Not exactly. Van couldn't say he felt the same about the other guy as he did about Kason, who'd held that title for years. In only a few short months, they were something different. Something more intense. It must have been because they shared so many intimate moments. Or maybe because they had such similar pasts.

He wasn't quite ready to name the feeling, but he'd be lying if he said they didn't share a special bond.

"Why are you looking at me like that?" Ollie asked.

"Like what?" Van sat up, crossed his arms, and put his back against the wall.

Kyra bridged the gap between them resting one hand on his knee and the other on Ollie's arm. "If he doesn't want to say it, I will. You were looking at him like you look at me sometimes. Like you give a shit."

"Because I do." Van couldn't believe she could still doubt it. "I meant it when I said I love you, Kyra. And Ollie is part of you."

"Ouch. For the record, I care about you for you." Ollie told Van, making him squirm. "And I don't mean that as a come on. I mean...unless you want me to mean it that way."

"Oh." Van had no idea what else to say.

Is that what he wanted? He couldn't deny that his cock was as hard as the other man's while they were having this discussion. But he'd never thought about having sex with a guy before.

Okay, he'd never really imagined he'd be in a committed threesome either.

What if...

"Do you mean to tell me you've never fooled around, even a little, with another guy?" Ollie cocked his head.

"Nope." Van shook his head.

"Not even exchanged a jerk off while sharing a dirty magazine when you were a teenager?" Ollie spread his hands wide like it would have been the most natural thing in the world if he had.

"Uh-uh."

"Or sucked your roommate off when they helped you with the bills and you were flat broke?"

"Jesus, Ollie. No."

As if he either wanted to see how far he could push Van or was investigating how judgey Van would be about Ollie's past, he kept escalating his *hypothetical* situations. "Let someone fuck you if you could fuck them back when you wondered what sex felt like but were too shy to talk to girls yet?"

"No way in hell!" Van sputtered.

He assumed Ollie was busting his balls as usual— until he realized the other guy wasn't cracking up at Van's obvious discomfort. He was dead serious. Shit! "Do people really do that stuff?"

"Uh, I did." Ollie scrubbed his hand over his face. "But maybe I'm just lame."

"You're not." Kyra jumped in then, rubbing Ollie's arm with reassuring strokes of her palm.

"I don't think so either." Van had to be sure the record was straight about that.

"Maybe people who wanted to take advantage could see that I was open to the possibility." Ollie shrugged. "Either way, it didn't seem like the worst way in the world to get stuff I needed, and I'm not going to lie, I enjoyed it too."

Van tried to hide his shock. "I guess because as long as I've known you, you've had a crush on Kyra, I never realized..."

"Does that make things weird for you?" Ollie asked quietly.

"Not at all. I just don't know what your expectations of me are." Van put his hands in his lap as if that would hide his boner.

"I don't have any. But if there's ever a time where you decide you'd like to try it, you have my permission to touch me however you like. Or ask me to do whatever you might want to experience."

"Thanks, but I'm good." Van's reaction was a reflex.

"Seriously? You're telling me you'd turn down the offer of a spectacular blowjob, just because it came from another man?" Ollie snorted. "You don't know what you're missing."

"Does that mean you'd show me?" Why the fuck had he said that? And why was his dick leaking precome at the thought?

Kyra interrupted. "Don't pressure him, Ollie. If it's not for him, it's not for him. That's fine. This isn't the sort of thing you should be doing on a dare or to try to prove that you're worldly. Whatever people choose to try freely between themselves, no problem. But coercion or challenge, nah. That's BS. *I'm* not into that."

"You're right." Ollie swallowed hard, then said, "Sorry, Van. I shouldn't have gotten so worked up. It's just that when you deny it like that, immediately and absolutely, it makes me feel like I was some kind of loser to do it or maybe there's something wrong with me for thinking the stuff I tried was no big deal."

"Never." Kyra hugged him.

"It's not that I'm ignorant or bigoted. It's new, that's all. I never thought of another dude that way." Van hesitated so long he thought Ollie would drop the subject. And then suddenly he was afraid the other man might. He couldn't deny that now that Ollie had put the idea in his mind, it was lingering. "Are you really offering to enlighten me?"

Kyra whipped around so fast she nearly toppled off the bed. Van grabbed her shoulder, then peered into her eyes as he asked, "Would you care if he did? Is that what had you so defensive?"

"Hell, no." Kyra grinned. "If you were into it, I'd love to see that. I didn't think..."

"Me either." Van said and shrugged one shoulder. "But never let it be said that I'm close-minded or unwilling to try new things. Get over here, Ollie."

He stroked his cock a few times, making it obvious he was in no way turned off by what they'd been discussing, wondering if the other guy would balk if he thought Van was serious. Maybe it had only been a bluff.

Nope. Ollie planted a kiss on Kyra's lips, then said, "Excuse me. I've got a dick to suck. Maybe you should give me some pointers. I might be kind of rusty."

Kyra giggled as Ollie hopped over her and zeroed in on Van's cock, licking his lips.

"Wait." Van put his hand on Ollie's shoulder so he couldn't quite reach his prize.

Ollie looked up, disappointment flashing in his eyes. "Change your mind?"

"No. I just want you to do this because *you* want to and for no other reason this time. No excuses. For either of us." Van leaned against the side of Ollie's home on wheels. He folded his hands behind his head, then said. "Go ahead. *If* you want to."

"Thanks," Ollie murmured, shifting something inside Van's chest. Suddenly this was more than some wild life experience, like the first time he'd tried sushi or gone bungee jumping. Ollie was important to him. As friends, sure. As his lover's lover, absolutely.

But maybe even deeper than that.

If they both loved Kyra, and planned to keep doing so together, they were going to have to be more than friends. They were going to be partners in life. And wouldn't it be better if they were more than simply co-partners?

Van probably would have thought a lot harder about it if Ollie's lips hadn't grazed the head of his cock right then —hot and wet and much less hesitant than any woman's that had ever been there before him.

Fuck!

Torn, and wrestling with the emotional aspect of what they were about to do, Van found his dick hadn't caught up entirely yet to where his mind had gone. Ollie took care of that, stroking him and tapping the tip of Van's still stiffening dick against his parted mouth as he nudged Van's thighs apart so he could reach between them to fondle Van's balls.

Kyra hummed as she scooched closer, leaning against his side for an up-close look at Ollie's ball-handling skills. She stared so intently he thought she might be studying every move the other man made. Van sure as shit wasn't going to complain about that. Because whatever the hell Ollie was doing to him felt better than any other hand or blowjob he could remember getting. If Kyra wanted to mimic his tricks, Van wasn't about to complain.

The teasing and light caresses were driving him mad. Without thinking about the implications, he reacted as his body demanded, burying one hand in Kyra's hair and the other in Ollie's. They weren't so different, both of their locks about the same length, wavy, and soft between his fingers.

Of course Van had fantasized about being with two partners before. He simply hadn't ever considered one of them might be another man. His fingers clenched in their hair.

"Yeah, you like it, don't you?" Ollie growled as he got more aggressive, obviously enjoying Van's possessive grasp. It seemed neither of them felt the need to be gentle with each other, which was fine with Van. Knowing he could let the dominant part of his nature have a little more chain turned him on.

"Fuck, yes." Van shifted, his ass clenched as he shoved his hips forward, urging Ollie to take him fully inside. "Enough playing. Suck me."

He probably should have said please, but having Kyra and Ollie teamed up and focused on his rapture drove him out of his mind. Kyra was smiling as she glanced between Ollie and Van like some sort of referee. Van appreciated having her there, considering how distracted he was. She would tell him if something went sideways with Ollie, freeing him to simply enjoy.

This could be even better than he'd ever imagined.

All thought about the possibilities flew from his mind when Ollie did as he was told. He parted his lips and went from licking and kissing the side of Van's shaft to engulfing the blunt cap of his cock. Even the moderate pressure he applied first made Van's toes curl and his head fall backward, where it clanged on the side of the van.

"Feels that good, huh?" Kyra asked with a chuckle.

"Uh huh." He tried to focus, looking down again in time to see his dick disappear between Ollie's lips. The man took him inside his mouth and then his throat with a single long glide that blew Van's mind. Women had often told him he had the biggest cock they'd seen in real life.

While he mostly thought they were flattering him, he couldn't deny that his previous partners had struggled to take all of him.

Ollie had no such problem.

"Son of a bitch!" he roared as the other man looked up with a wicked glint in his eyes and then began to suck.

If Van didn't last at least a minute, he'd never live it down. But with Ollie about to suck the come straight from his balls, he wasn't holding out a lot of hope for a lengthy performance.

The other man bobbed over Van's cock, adding an up-and-down motion to whatever the fuck his tongue and cheeks and throat were doing. On his upstrokes, he used his hands to fill the gap between his lips and Van's balls before descending and engulfing him in strong, wet heat once again.

Kyra cooed at Ollie, "That's so sexy. Damn, you're good at that."

When she leaned forward, Van slacked his grip on her hair enough that she could kiss Ollie's cheek, making the other man smile and choke as she distracted him.

Van didn't blame the guy. Besides, he needed a break or he was going to embarrass himself for sure.

He tugged on Ollie's hair, making him flick his gaze toward Van. "Kiss her. I want to watch you make out. Let her taste my dick on your lips."

"Fuck, yeah. Do that," Kyra echoed.

Ollie lifted off Van with a sound that would be synonymous with sex in Van's brain for the rest of his life. Then he parted his lips and waited for Kyra to come to him as if afraid she might not accept him or want him after what he'd done.

Yeah, right.

Kyra lunged for him, slanting her mouth over Ollie's reddened one. She kissed him so deeply, Van thought she might suffocate. Their tongues clashed. They moaned and writhed closer to one another until Van couldn't stand watching and not participating a moment longer.

His cock ached. It stood between them, a drop of pearlescent fluid rolling down the head. He swore he'd never been as hard as he was at that moment. "The two of you are so fucking hot. I can't stand it. Get back over here, Ollie."

When he broke away from Kyra, breathing hard, Ollie grinned at her and she reflected it right back at him. "You'd better do as he says. This looks painful."

She eyed his cock and hummed. Any other time, Van would have grabbed her, flipped her around so she was on her hands and knees, then plunged inside her tight pussy and fucked until he flooded her sweet body with his release. Not right then, though.

Because Ollie was working his magic again. The guy groaned and devoured Van, shocking him all over again with the full intensity of his fellatio skills. His tongue caressed the underside of Van's shaft even as his mouth increased the suction.

It wasn't another minute before Van was on the brink of losing control.

Until Kyra saved him. Again.

Was she doing it on purpose? Could she tell he was about to blow?

"Could I have a taste, Ollie?" she whispered in their lover's ear, and he nodded, edging Van closer to his orgasm. Then he pulled off and gasped, drawing in two lungfuls of air.

He fisted Van's dick and aimed it toward Kyra, who was

a lot more delicate when she licked the head then slipped him into her mouth. She didn't even attempt to swallow all of him. They knew she wasn't able to manage it. The contrast of her finesse with Ollie's raw passion made Van squirm.

He cursed when Ollie took the opportunity to slide in beneath her. First he nuzzled Van's balls and then he licked a line up the center of his sack. Finally, he opened his mouth and began to lave Van's nuts. By the time he started sucking on them in time to Kyra's motions, Van knew he was in trouble. There was no stopping it this time.

"Oh shit. I'm close." He used his grip on Kyra's hair, which he hadn't been able to let go of, to pull her off, and then guided Ollie's head back to where it belonged. The man was made to suck cock.

Van's cock. At least right then.

"Make him come, Ollie." Kyra cheered him on. "I can't wait to see him shoot down your throat. I want to see you wreck him and show him exactly how good it can be. You're amazing. Watching you go down on him makes me so horny. You know I'm going to fuck you, right? I need your dick in me soon. So hurry up and finish him. Please."

Neither Van nor Ollie was capable of denying her.

Van had never heard something as sinfully erotic as Kyra's dirty stream of consciousness. And whether he admitted it or not, the idea of watching her and Ollie fuck was just as arousing as Ollie's spectacular oral. Or close, anyway.

Van roared. "Yes! Suck it. So good. I'm going to give you what you want, Ollie."

That last part he hadn't meant to say, but it came out anyway. Just like the fluid that began to spurt from his cock and into Ollie's mouth. If the other guy minded, he didn't say so. Instead, he did as Van said and sucked and sucked and sucked.

The orgasm that smashed into Van was more powerful than anything he could have anticipated. He tensed all over then bucked, fucking Ollie's mouth as the man drew every last drop of come from his balls. Kyra's encouragement and the caresses of her hands over his jerking muscles kept him grounded when he might have otherwise freaked out.

He was coming harder than he had in his entire life, for a man. For Ollie.

And fuck if it didn't feel incredible.

Van felt his abs shuddering as he emptied himself completely. He would have sworn he was glowing from the inside out, his very bones filled with light, having shared this experience with Kyra, his lover, and the man who was quickly earning a similar designation.

Replete, he went slack everywhere, sliding down the concave wall of the van until he was slung across Ollie's bed. His foot accidentally connected with Ollie's phone, which hit the floor with a crunch. "Oh shit! Sorry."

"Oops!" Kyra grabbed the device from the floor and handed it to Ollie with a wince.

"I'll take it as a compliment." Ollie grinned despite the obvious damage to his cell phone's camera, which had cracked. "I'm too worn out, and horny, to worry about it now."

He had put on a hell of a show.

As Van struggled to calm his racing heart before it exploded, Ollie collapsed as well, rubbing his jaw as he extended a hand to Kyra, who clasped it in hers, kissing his knuckles.

For a few minutes, they were quiet, the only noise inside the cozy home on wheels the sound of their ragged breathing with the rush of traffic passing the arena in the background.

"Van." Kyra nudged him, as if making sure he was still alive after he'd come so hard.

"Huh?"

"You know what's polite after someone gives you the best blowjob of your life?" she asked, reminding him that he had two other partners to consider even if he was still flying on the high of his climax.

"Turnabout?" he asked, opening one eye.

19

"**Y**ou don't have to do that." Ollie jerked upright, peeling himself off of Van's thighs, where he'd been recovering after such a stellar performance. "You said this wasn't like those other times. This wasn't a blowjob in exchange for something. It was just 'cause I wanted to suck your big fat dick. It's been a while and I thought it would be fun to corrupt you."

"Damn, Ollie." Van felt desire stirring even though he'd so recently threatened to blow Ollie's head off with the force of his orgasm. But for what? How far did he want to take things? "I'm not sure I'm ready, or any kind of an expert..."

"Seriously, that's fine." Ollie grimaced as he resituated himself, his cock clearly visible despite the sheet he pulled over his lap. It had to be uncomfortable to be that hard. "I'm going to hit the shower. I'll take care of myself then be right back."

"No!" both Kyra and Van shouted simultaneously.

Ollie froze, staring between them.

"Come here," Kyra coaxed, holding out her hand.

It would have been easy to let her take his burden, but Van wasn't one to foist his debts off on someone else. Besides, there was that pesky matter of his dick, which was twitching against his leg like it wanted to get in on the action, even if Ollie's epic performance had made that impossible at the moment.

"You don't have to either," Ollie told her.

"If you don't fool around with me right now I'm going to die. So there's that." Kyra growled as she launched herself over Van's legs and tackled Ollie. "Besides, I *want* to. Unless you're not into it with a woman right now. Or with me specifically..." She hesitated.

Van was about to shake her, to make her see what he did—how desirable she was and how desperately both he and Ollie needed her. How could she still doubt it?

Fortunately, Ollie agreed. He locked his arms around her waist so she couldn't retreat and then angled his head and kissed her.

Van couldn't stop staring, wondering if he was supposed to be jealous. Of Ollie or even of Kyra after what had just gone down. Literally.

Except he wasn't.

He was so glad that Ollie was ready and more than willing to take care of Kyra.

Maybe he was lazy or simply dazed from how Ollie had altered everything he thought he knew about himself and what he liked, but he doubted he could have moved right then, never mind launched the sweet assault Ollie did on their girl.

Their girl.

Huh.

It was impossible to deny as Van lounged there and witnessed their interactions. Somehow, this had become a thing. And not some kind of temporary hook up either. Van's whole world changed as he soaked in ultimate satisfaction. Physical, yes. But more than that. Emotional and mental, too.

Because he knew now what he and Kyra had been missing, why things hadn't progressed on their own even after years of solid friendship.

Ollie. He was the key to making them work.

Overcome with affection and longing, Van rolled onto his side and ran his hand down Kyra's back, admiring the curve of her hips and her lush, spankable ass. And when his hand meandered upward to her shoulder, he didn't stop there. He cupped Ollie's cheek, rubbing his thumb in an arc beside where he was making out with Kyra.

Van's digit pressed against that seal and they turned as one, taking it into their mouths. They swirled their tongues around it and each other.

That was it. He needed to see them do more than kiss.

Van got to his knees and started pulling off the remaining covers. They sighed when they had to stop kissing in order for him to shove aside the soft material but then came back together twice as passionately when it was removed.

Ollie palmed Kyra's exposed breasts. Van tried to help. He reached between them to palm Kyra's mound. When his hand accidentally brushed Ollie's stiff cock, they both gasped. Their stares snapped to each other as if they were magnetic. Ollie's eyes widened and darkened.

"I'm almost there," Van promised. "Let me get her ready for you to fuck."

"She's ready!" Kyra shouted, her nails digging into Ollie's shoulders. "Let's go."

Van chuckled and so did Ollie.

Though not for long, because Van's hand turned and cupped Ollie's cock. If his fingers curled the slightest bit, finding out what it felt like to hold another man's dick in his hand, he didn't think anyone could fault his curiosity.

Ollie shuddered and arched. He groaned to Kyra, "I need to be inside you."

"Yes." She moaned as she planted her hands on Ollie's chest, knocking him to his back, then climbed over him so she could rub her pussy along the length of his cock.

"Then let's get him in that nice, tight pussy of yours," Van said as he positioned himself behind Kyra, in between Ollie's spread legs. "He did such a good job sucking me off. Don't you think he deserves a reward?"

"Yeah." Kyra nodded, biting her lower lip.

"You're going to have his cock, baby. Don't worry. I've got you." Van inched closer until her back was plastered against his chest. He wrapped an arm around her waist and lifted her barely enough that he had room to slip his hand between them.

Ollie reached for his own cock, but Van stopped him with a glare. "Put your hands at your sides. Lay there and enjoy."

"Yes, sir," he quipped. The joke fell flat in the face of the very real power exchange they'd somehow fallen into.

Van wasn't complaining. He was finally able to free a part of himself he'd always restrained. Maybe not so different from Ollie after all.

He kissed the side of Kyra's neck and murmured, "Is that okay? If I use you to fuck him? Is that what you want, too?"

Kyra shivered in his hold. "If you don't, I'll be pissed."

Van laughed and Ollie relaxed. He honestly still didn't

get it. What was wrong with his amazing lovers that they didn't see how extraordinary he knew them to be?

He wasn't sure, but he showed Ollie how much Kyra wanted him. He wrapped his hand around Ollie's cock, measuring it with a pump or two before directing it toward Kyra's opening. He fit them together then lowered her, joining their bodies as tightly as their desires aligned.

A moan fell from Kyra's parted lips and her eyes rolled back as Van allowed her to sink onto Ollie, embedding him within her.

"Fuck, yes." Ollie grunted and rocked his hips upward, burrowing deeper into Kyra's moist heat.

So Van gave them what they craved. He pressed Kyra lower until she took all of Ollie within her and her pussy rested on his torso. Breath wheezed from her as her body stretched to accommodate him. After a few seconds, she began to grind on him, rubbing her clit against his pubic bone.

Ollie cursed, then looked to Van. "Can I play with her clit?"

"You better. I want her to come so hard she wrings you dry." Van held her tighter.

He grasped Kyra's hips and raised then lowered her, using her body to fuck Ollie. She didn't seem to mind in the least. In fact, she threw her head back against his shoulder and looked up at him, studying the intensity on his face as he did his best to make sure Ollie was satisfied.

That's when he noticed the other man staring at them.

"What?" Van asked. "What do you want?"

"Kiss her. Let me watch while she fucks me. I love that. Please." Ollie strained on the bed, fucking into Kyra even as Van lowered her over him. Who was he to deny the man?

He captured Kyra's lips with a growl, enjoying facilitating their pleasure. Both hers and Ollie's. And, he realized, his own. Because bringing them bliss was giving him a hell of a lot of his own.

Ollie groaned and fisted the sheets. He clung to the bed as if he might rocket off the mattress if he wasn't careful. Van tried to ramp him up even more by making out with Kyra, who melted in his arms. She kissed him back, her eyes wide open as she smiled against his lips.

He separated them just enough to murmur, "You like this?"

"Fucking love it. The two of you are better than porn." She bit his jaw then, waiting for him to return to feasting on her lips.

He was still kissing her when she began to tremble in his grasp. Ollie must have felt the change in her too. He warned Van, "She's getting tighter on me. Going to come all over me."

"Hell, yes she is." Van hoped they understood it was a command. "And you're going to come with her."

"Don't think I could resist." Ollie panted, clearly already struggling to hold back his orgasm.

Van helped him out as best he could by leaning down and taking Kyra's nipple in his mouth. He bit lightly on her flesh, toying with her piercing. As he expected, that set her off.

She screamed Ollie's name and then Van's as she jerked in his arms.

He held her tight and watched as Ollie erupted within her, pumping his release into the woman they loved so much. Before he'd even finished, he held his arms up and open.

Van carefully lowered Kyra into them. Their lover

cradled her on his chest. But then he looked over her shoulder, directly at Van.

Though Ollie didn't ask him to join them, Van could see that he would like it. So he did without making Ollie beg. He stretched out beside Kyra and Ollie, putting one arm around Kyra's back, against Ollie's knotted forearm.

When Ollie looked over at him and said, "Thank you," something in Van snapped.

The other guy should realize he'd been the star of this show and instead he was acting like Van had given him something unbelievably special by accepting a blowjob and treating him with respect. That was fucked up.

His instincts drove him to respond and without thinking too hard about what they were telling him. Van leaned in and locked his mouth over Ollie's. Kyra sighed and squirmed on him. Her pussy still hugged his half-hard cock, making the other guy groan into Van's mouth. Or at least he assumed that's what caused the rush of pleasure that burst from his chest in a strangled moan.

Kyra said, "Holy shit. You're making me come again. Kiss him, Van. Kiss the shit out of him."

Van discovered that he liked her urging them on. He deepened his kiss with Ollie, finding it odd and also wondrous when the other man's beard scratched his face as they ate at each other. The first taste was interesting, the second intoxicating, and after that, he couldn't seem to get enough.

Damn. He'd just come. So he couldn't even use horniness as some kind of justification.

No, the truth was, he liked kissing Ollie. Liked it a lot.

Kyra caressed them all over, running her fingers through their hair and telling them repeatedly how much they moved her. Van did the same, stroking her back and then up Ollie's arm, which was wrapped possessively around Kyra where she was draped over him.

Van couldn't believe it when he felt his cock hardening again. He tried to back off and calm down, but neither Ollie nor Kyra was having any of that.

"Don't run now," Kyra whispered in his ear.

That wasn't what he was doing. Was it?

Van didn't want either of them to think he wasn't all in on whatever it was they were doing, redirecting the course of his life in a direction he'd never imagined possible. He grabbed Kyra's hip then lightly shoved until she realized what he wanted. She slid off Ollie, letting his cock slip from her body before she nestled into his side.

Ollie groaned, though he didn't object for long because Van took her place. He tried not to crush Ollie except the other man wrapped his arm around Van's waist and kept him close when Van would have lifted off and given him room to breathe. That meant their cocks made contact, rubbing against each other as they got situated.

Van was relieved to feel Ollie was as stiff as he was despite his recent orgasm. He was into it too.

Kyra knocked her loose fist into the side of Van's ass. He hadn't realized how clenched his muscles were until her knuckles bounced off it. She got his attention long enough to say, "Lift up a little. Just a little."

So he planted his knees and put an inch of space between their pelvises.

He didn't have time to mourn the loss of the heat of Ollie's dick or the impression it had been making on his abs because Kyra reached between them and surrounded their cocks with her hand. Or at least, she tried. She couldn't quite grip all of them.

Instead, she used the flat of her palm to trap their

hard-ons between it and Ollie's abs, which were flexing as he clenched his jaw and writhed beneath Van's bulk. Kyra asked, "Better?"

Both of them rasped some sort of assent, even if actual words were too difficult to muster given the euphoria threatening to drown him.

Van couldn't stay still any longer. He rocked his hips, causing his cock to travel along the length of Ollie's and his balls to drag across Ollie's sack. Kyra squeezed them together, making Van grunt.

It was half-handjob and half-humping. Van didn't give a shit what it was called, he kept doing it faster and faster until he was frantically pumping in search of release.

Someday, he'd have enough self-control to fuck Ollie right. To sink into his ass and possess the man while ensuring his pleasure. But he didn't know enough yet to make sure he didn't hurt Ollie and he wasn't about to stop for even the two seconds it would take to flip the man over and drill inside his tight hole.

Thinking about it was enough. Van roared. He leaned down and bit Ollie's shoulder in a frantic show of possession that seemed to set Ollie off too.

Van wasn't sure who surrendered first, but suddenly both of them were icing Ollie's chest, Kyra's hand, and each other's dicks.

"Son of a bitch!" Kyra lunged for the T-shirt Van had left on the counter near the bed the night before in order to clean Ollie up. "You two made quite the mess. You must not have hated that, huh?"

She was grinning at them both while her hands wandered over her body. One began to rub her pussy while the other pulled at her piercings.

Neither Ollie nor Van was going to allow her to take care of herself after their own decadence.

Ollie looked at Van and said, "You want to eat her or should I?"

"I'm always hungry for you," Van told Kyra, then carefully covered her.

"But..." She squirmed out of his hold, or tried, when his mouth approached the apex of her thighs.

"What?" He tipped his head as he studied her reactions.

"Ollie already came in me. I'm dirty." She blushed furiously despite everything they'd done together.

"Switch places, Van. I don't mind." Ollie tapped Van's shoulder.

"Hell, no. Neither do I." He buried his face in her folds and lapped Ollie's release from her skin. Van hoped someday they'd understand that their shared love wasn't some kind of imposition and it sure as hell didn't make her less desirable. It was how they worked. How they were meant to be and he planned to embrace that every day of his life from then on.

Ollie whispered a string of curses in Spanish before descending on Kyra. He cradled her while kissing her softly and toying with her breasts and the bars through her nipples. Van pressed three fingers deep into her clenching sheath, glad for the lubrication Ollie had left behind.

When he scissored them, spreading her apart, Kyra clamped down around him.

Ollie moaned into her mouth. "I love you, Kyra. *We* love you. Come for us."

She did.

Her body spasmed so hard that she nearly broke his

fingers. And he wouldn't have complained even if she had. Her climax seemed to last forever, jolting her with shock after shock of pleasure.

Before they could really soak it in and talk about what had happened, a loud triple bang came at the door. Kason yelled, "If you're all done now, we need Kyra on stage to test the new lighting set up with her drum kit."

"Fuck you!" she shouted.

"Sounds like Van and Ollie did it for me," he teased. "Take your time, but we do need you when you can walk again."

Kyra groaned, making Ollie and Van crack up.

The best sex of his life and laughter too?

Van was in heaven.

20

O llie hung around backstage as Kason, Kyra, and the rest of the band got ready for their show. It was the last one before the holidays and only a few hundred miles from Middletown, so some of their Hot Rods and Hot Rides friends had come to support the band. That included Walker and Dane, who'd take any excuse to ride their motorcycles, even in the freezing weather.

They were hanging out with him in the lounge area while roadies zoomed this way and that, hauling equipment, shouting, and generally getting shit done. Kyra was sitting next to him, waiting for the crew to finish rigging some new lighting so she could do her sound check.

Van, who used to guard Kason primarily, had reassigned himself. Especially in light of the Number One incidents, the security team had agreed it was best that Kyra have a dedicated bodyguard. Besides, Jordan clearly was sticking by Kason's side from now on, so they'd shuffled roles and everyone seemed good with that.

As much as Ollie had come to enjoy Walker and Dane's company since they'd joined the shop, he sort of wished he was alone with Kyra and Van so they could talk openly about what had happened earlier that morning and where it left them. For his part, there wasn't even a shred of doubt.

In fact... He opened his mouth before he considered how embarrassing it would be if Kyra and Van didn't like his idea.

"You know, there are two sides to this pendant my mami made me." He withdrew it from beneath his shirt, smiling as the impact of his treasure hit him all over again. "Maybe I could take a picture of you to put in there. Would you mind?"

"Oh, Ollie, that's so sweet. I'd be honored." Kyra stood and attempted to finger-comb her hair into some semblance of order. "Where do you want to take it?"

On the other hand, Van stepped aside.

"Where are you going?" Ollie wondered.

"Me?" Van seemed surprised. "You want me in the picture, too?"

Ollie's face fell. Had he misunderstood what had gone down earlier? Had it only been physical to Van? "I mean, not if you don't want to be. I'm not going to force you or anything. I sort of thought after...you know...that we were in this together. All the way. Was I wrong?"

Kyra whipped a glare to Van. Ollie wished she hadn't. Similar to how Van hadn't pressured him, he didn't want to force the other guy to give more than he was ready to offer freely.

"No." Van held his hands up, palms out. "I didn't mean it like it seemed. I just... Yeah, I want to be in the picture."

Ollie wasn't sure anymore that it was a good idea. But selfishly, he still had the urge to memorialize what had been a special occasion to him. "Okay, scoot together then. This thing isn't very big. I'll have to crop the image pretty tight."

He held up his cell, then groaned. "Ah, shit. I forgot the camera on my phone is busted."

"Use mine." Kyra took her phone from her back pocket, unlocked it, then tossed it to him. He caught it with one hand. When he looked down, he said, "Oops, I hit something. I'm in your texts, I think."

His brows drew together as he spotted something that looked suspicious and tapped it. "Kyra...what the fuck?"

"Oh shit. Wait! Don't—" Kyra lunged for her phone in a maneuver worthy of a mother who walks into the kitchen when their child is about to touch a hot stove.

"Why?" Ollie grimaced as he saw what was in her messages.

"What is it?" Van snatched the device from him, his own frown emerging. "Who the hell's dick is this? It's not mine. And it isn't Ollie's—"

"You know what Ollie's dick looks like?" Dane asked, earning himself a glare from everyone in the room and a whack from the back of Walker's hand in his gut. "*Oof.*"

Van refused to be deterred. For that matter, so did Ollie.

"I don't care that you have a dick pic on your phone," he told Kyra. "That's an Iowa number and a profession of undying love. I'm more worried about the fact that it seems like Number One could have been sending you messages and you never mentioned it. The date on that is from weeks ago. Why the fuck didn't you tell us about it?"

"What?" Van's face went straight past red to full on purple. If he had been a cartoon, steam would have poured out his ears.

"Uh oh," Dane said right before he and Walker wandered off, shooing everyone else from a hundred foot radius to give them some relative privacy.

"So you really don't trust us, do you?" Ollie blinked at her, trying to ignore the one-two punch she and Van had landed on his heart. He'd been wrong to make himself vulnerable again. Because all it did was lead to getting hurt.

"That's not why I didn't say anything. I got the message that day, right before we slept together the first time, and I didn't want to ruin the mood. Then I tried to tell you but Kason interrupted, calling us home so I thought it was bad timing. He never contacted me again, so I thought it wasn't worth mentioning. We already increased security and I've been with you and Van every minute since then." Kyra tried to explain, but it was hard to imagine any excuse would be adequate.

She obviously didn't understand what it would do to him if something bad happened to her. It was too risky. He'd been dumb to fall for someone that selfish.

And starting to do the same with Van, someone who openly admitted he'd never been attracted to a man before, well...that had been twice as moronic.

Ollie was asking to get ripped apart.

He stumbled backward a step.

Kyra reached for him, clutching his hand. "You told me you wouldn't let go until I asked. I'm not asking yet. Please listen."

He couldn't. He was done heeding his heart or his

dick. Both were leading him into a dangerous place. It was better to escape half broken than to wait any longer and risk setting himself back twenty years.

Ollie pried Kyra's fingers off his hand, then shook his head. "I'm sorry. No. I can't. It's obvious now that this isn't what I thought. With either of you. I'm out."

~

KYRA WASN'T proud of the wail that tore from her throat.

That didn't keep her from trying to salvage the situation.

"I'm so sorry, Van. I fucked up, okay?" She hated herself for it, but she began to cry. "That doesn't mean it's okay for you to stomp on Ollie's heart, too. It hurt him when you didn't realize he wanted you in his picture because you mean something to him and he hopes that someday he might mean something to you too."

"Son of a bitch!" Van scrunched his eyes closed. "He does. Already. I'm still getting used to it, though. I never expected that."

"Then please, go after him. Bring him back and then maybe we can fix this. I'll understand if you don't want to be with me anymore, but at least treat Ollie right. Please. Tell him you care since he's not about to believe I do anymore."

"I don't know, Kyra. If it's not about us three, then...I don't know." Van clasped his skull between his hands as if he had a monster headache. "We never would have been more than friends if not for you. If it's not all three of us, I don't think it works. I won't give him the wrong idea or fuck things up more than they already are."

"You're making the same mistake with him that you made with me. And if you hurt him and lose him over this, for us both, I'm going to have a hard time forgiving you." Kyra was equal parts pissed off for Ollie and pissed off *at* herself.

"I guess that makes two of us then. Doing the same old shit, I mean. I don't give a fuck what you told Ollie about why—you had plenty of opportunity to inform us about that creepy ass text. And you didn't." Van glared at her, crossing his arms as if that could protect them from the ways they hurt each other.

Kyra wanted to protest. To say that she'd been afraid of spooking Ollie by letting him think she was in danger or triggering Van, who would assume she didn't have faith that he would protect her simply because she hadn't brought it up the instant it happened. And once she'd waited long enough to be sure it was a one-off message... well, it was too late to change the fact that she hadn't disclosed it immediately.

Neither Ollie nor Van could understand what it was like to be a woman in the public eye and how dick pics were an annoying side effect of what moderate fame she had as a background performer on the fringes of Kason's success. It wasn't *that* unusual for her inbox to be hit with one.

"I promise. I will never do this again. I swear I've learned my lesson, Van." Kyra was desperate. "Just please, go find Ollie. Bring him back. Don't let him get too far away before you convince him that we need him, even if we suck at showing it. If you two will give me another chance, I'll do everything I can to deserve it this time. Please."

Van stared between her and the door Ollie had stormed out of. "I don't know about all of that. But whatever happens, he shouldn't be driving when he's upset. It would kill me if something happened to him because what I said or did impaired him. Stay inside the arena. Do not under any circumstances go anywhere alone. If you don't want me with you, you call Jordan and he'll get one of the other security guards. Do you understand?"

She nodded.

"Say it, Kyra. And mean it." Van went stone cold as he looked at her. "I won't ever trust you again if you lie to me now."

"I understand." Her shoulders sagged.

Then he shouted, "Fuck!" before jogging after their lover, leaving her to wonder if she'd ruined everything they'd almost had.

Silent tears dripped off her chin as she stood there, devastated.

She didn't know how long she'd been frozen in place except that her legs were numb. Walker approached her slowly, speaking as carefully as if she was a wild animal he was trying to tame. "Kyra...why don't you come sit down? Do you want me to call Wren or Devra or anyone else to talk to you?"

"No." Her lips felt cold, so unlike they had when she'd kissed Ollie and Van mere hours ago. She turned and stumbled toward the stage.

"Where are you going?" Dane asked her.

"Don't worry. I'm not leaving. I'm staying inside like Van ordered. I just..." She shook her head. "I'm going to take out my frustrations on my poor drums. That's fucking allowed, isn't it?"

"Yeah. Yeah, go ahead." Walker watched her go. "I'm sure your guys will be back soon."

Kyra wasn't so sure about that. If they were willing to throw everything they'd had away over one stupid mistake, they really must not love her the way she loved them.

Because this...this felt like she was dying inside.

21

Kyra sat in the dark arena. She gripped her drumsticks, one in each fist. Afraid they would shatter if she squeezed them any harder, she forced herself to relax each finger. And when she'd done that, she worked her way up her arms, rotating her wrists, then stretching her forearms and shoulders.

The only way she was going to survive the night, their show, and the rest of the disaster her life had become was if she could calm down, stop panicking, and think rationally, which she definitely had not been doing a few minutes ago.

Although she didn't usually take her full practice session on days they performed live, she was going to make an exception. Playing would vent some of her discordant emotions, turning the jagged edges inside her into motion and energy and sound.

Ugliness would become beautiful.

Thankfully, she'd built up enough stamina over the years that she'd probably still be able to make it through the entire set list that evening, even if she'd need one hell of a massage the next morning. Having a masseuse on staff was a perk Kason had insisted on for all of them once they'd reached the big leagues.

The roadies hadn't yet finished setting up the personal lights she used to illuminate her kit and the area near her during dark parts of the concert. So she stood and fumbled around the base of the new spotlight rig that had been partially assembled before she'd cleared the stage so she could mope in solitude. It was standing and plugged in, so she figured it would be fine for the half hour or so she planned to take out her anger on the drums.

The longer she spent in the aftermath of the spectacular collapse of her budding relationship, the more she was willing to admit it wasn't rage or disappointment fueling her turmoil. Fear. That's what clawed at her guts like bad Mexican food.

Because she knew that if she lost Van or Ollie or both, she'd never find a connection like they had again in her lifetime. This was it. They were it for her.

Whether they fucking realized it or not.

Idiots! Herself included, for giving them any reason to doubt the sincerity or depth of her emotions.

Kyra huffed out a breath, flipped on the breaker for the light stand, and watched as a beam brighter than the summer sun blasted down to illuminate her drums. If she sat there in the center of it and played, maybe everything else would fade away like the rest of the arena beyond the stage already had.

She hoped so.

Sitting down again, she cradled her sticks in her hands this time, stroking them lovingly before tapping out a beat on the bass drum with her foot.

She couldn't say much about what happened after

that. As usual, rhythms took over her body. They morphed and expanded as she toyed with them, always trying to play them cleaner, faster, or more originally. And next thing she knew, she was blasting through her featured solo, which gave Kason a chance to take a break and rehydrate during the show.

Kyra tinkered with it, improving bits as her skills and tastes evolved. When she was out of breath, and her eyes burned with the sweat dripping into them, she stopped, letting the final crash of a cymbal ring through the air and her soul.

Adrenaline coursed through her, making her heart pound and the breath saw in and out of her lungs. It was nearly as potent as the orgasms she'd experienced while trapped between Ollie and Van. Nearly.

She lowered her sticks and sat there, panting and sweating. Kind of pissed that her first thought after she finished playing was of the two people she'd been trying to beat out of her system. *Fuck.*

A string of applause from a single person echoed through the space. She snapped her head up, suddenly regretting the lights, which blinded her to her surroundings. All she could see was the hint of a silhouette, backlit by an open door far, far away. The man was too tall to be Ollie and too skinny to be Van.

"Who's there?" she asked.

"Your number one fan."

No. It couldn't be.

"I can't believe you're in here, practicing before the show. You never do that."

"I can't believe you're in here. Period. It's a little weird that you know so much about what I do, Number One." Okay, *a little* was the understatement of the century. But maybe he really was a socially inept man-child who didn't realize how he came off.

"Sorry, I'm super awkward." He came nearer so she could discern a few more details of him like his unkempt hair. Then he sniffed and wiped his nose on his sleeve. "That's one reason I like you so much. You're cool."

Kyra surrendered a twisted laugh at that. "Hardly, but thanks."

Maybe he wasn't so bad after all.

"So how'd you get in here anyway?" she asked, trying to stall in the hopes that someone would come by for a sound check or to test out the lighting despite her earlier tirade about how they should stay the fuck out until she told them they could come back. There was little to no solitude in their business. Of course today they seemed to realize she was a woman on the edge and had taken her seriously.

"Oh, I'm always the first person in. I wouldn't be your number one fan if I wasn't first." He ambled closer still, to the very edge of the stage so she caught the sharp angle of his nose and the thick brows above dark eyes. Then he lowered his voice conspiratorially, having exactly the opposite effect on Kyra that he had been hoping for. She stood and rounded her kit so she wasn't trapped by the instruments, edging toward the wings and the partially completed riggings there.

"Of course. You're right." She tried to smile, though it must have come out crooked. "You go to all our shows, don't you? That takes commitment."

"You don't even understand." He puffed up at that, as if she'd been complimenting him instead of wondering how unbalanced that made him. "I've had to do some things— bad things—to get the money to do this. It's not cheap. I try to take buses when I can, but sometimes the shows are too close together and I have to fly. Plus I have to buy tickets to every concert and whatever the last performance is before yours at each arena so I can sleep in the bathrooms and make sure I get in here first. Before everyone else."

And there it was. That over-the-top factor. She tried to sound unfazed as she backed away, inching closer to the exit. "Wow, that's...intense, Number One. What's your real name, anyway? Where are you from?"

"I'm nobody and not from anywhere important." He shrugged. "But...there's something I read online and I was wondering if it was true. Do you have a boyfriend now?"

Maybe all she had to do was say yes and he'd back off. Okay, not likely, but it was about the only chance she had. So she took it. "Yeah. His name is Van and he's ginormous. The head of security. I'm sure you remember seeing him around at the meet-and-greets."

"That meathead?" Number One flung his hands out and let them drop. "Come on, you're better than that, Kyra."

"No, I've loved him for a long time. We've been friends forever and recently...things got even more amazing between us." She couldn't say why she was telling him except that it was true. She hoped Van believed it as completely as Number One seemed to.

In fact, she might have laid it on a bit thick for his liking.

"What about me? I've done all this for you. Given you everything I have and more. Stuff that wasn't even mine. I've slept in the streets for you. Cheered so loud I ruined my voice." That explained the unnatural rasp.

"I'm sorry that happened to you." She was, truly.

Horrified, even. Number One needed help. She wasn't angry at him. Just sad. And, fine, scared shitless.

Where was Van? Was he coming back? Why hadn't he come to check on her? Probably because he thought she was safely ensconced in the heart of the arena.

He never would have thought someone could get through his rings of protection.

Because they couldn't.

Unless they were there before the barriers went up.

Shit.

"I'm not. I'm not sorry at all. You're worth it. But if you have a boyfriend now, then none of it matters. I should give up. What's the point of living if I can't have you?"

"Hang on. Don't say things like that. There's plenty of reasons." Kyra didn't know how to walk this line. She was terrified for herself and for Number One. She couldn't live with it on her conscience if he did something to harm himself.

"Name one." He wrung his hands as he climbed onto the stage with uncoordinated and labored movements. She retreated some more, her shoulder knocking one of the metal light stands. Startled, she dropped her sticks. Her only possible weapon rolled toward Number One, making her curse herself.

"How about a private concert for you alone?"

"You just gave me one."

"Yeah, but now I know you're here. It won't be practice, but the real thing. How about it?"

"Okay. Play for me," he demanded, plucking her sticks from the ground, caressing them reverently, then handing them back to her. With her only chance at freedom presented to her, she reached out and grabbed them.

She tried to buy herself some time. If she started

playing again, Van or the roadies or whoever else would stay away, like she'd told them to. If it was quiet, maybe they'd come see what was up or if they could continue their work.

"Like you said, I never practice before the show. If I play more right now, I'll be too tired to make it through the whole set list. You wouldn't want that, would you?" She tried to reason with him, already knowing it was futile. His eyes were wide and dark, no reason to be found in their depths.

"I don't care about everyone else. I'm finally going to get what I've always wanted. What I've been too scared to ask for." He grinned, showing off uneven teeth that had been the victim of years of neglect and poor hygiene.

This man needed her help. She tried once more. "Okay, what if I play one song for you now? Then will you let me take you backstage and show you around? Introduce you to the rest of the band..."

And security.

"Oh no." He shook his head vehemently. "I don't care about them either. Only you. Once you start playing, you won't be able to stop. I want you to play and play and play. For me. Forever. No more chasing you every night. No more bad things. No more. I can finally rest and have you all to myself."

"No one can play forever." She laughed until she realized he was dead serious. He thought she was the key to escaping his obsessive behaviors. No wonder he was so insistent. So...unrelenting.

"You will. Do it. Play for me. And if you stop—please, please don't stop—because then bad things will happen to you, too." The steel with which he promised it made her sure he meant it.

"Number One, I'm tired. I need to rest. I—" She stopped short of saying she had a horrible day, because compared to his...was it really?

Right then and there Kyra realized she'd been a moron. Absolutely irrational in her own way. And as soon as she got the chance to tell Van and Ollie that she would respect them and whatever they needed to feel secure in her love from then on, she was going to make them believe it was true.

Kyra would have backed up again but she couldn't go any farther. In fact, her foot landed on top of the coiled wires that led up to the incredibly powerful stage lights. It plunged into the pile and got tangled, throwing her slightly off balance.

Number One was out of patience or maybe sanity. He was terrified for himself and for her.

That made both of them.

"PLAY FOR ME!" he roared in that shredded voice.

It sent shivers up her spine and flash froze her heart. She reacted on a base, instinctual level.

"Like hell I will." Kyra lunged at him, using one of her sticks as a weapon. If she could stun him or injure him, maybe she could dart past him and escape. Why had she sent Van away and refused anyone else? Hell, Walker or Dane would have sat quietly and kept her company. A couple of badass bikers would have done the trick nicely.

She was done with stupid mistakes and bad decisions.

When she got out of this mess, if she got out of it, she was going to quit being so afraid of asking for help that she put herself in these situations.

Unfortunately, Number One was shockingly nimble or high on adrenaline. He dodged her attack then grasped her wrist, twisting it until she had no choice but to drop and roll to avoid breaking her bones. That could be the end of her career and everything she'd always dreamed of...until Ollie and Van, at least.

As she tumbled, her boot yanked the cord it was caught in. And before she knew it, one of the giant stands holding the fancy lights, which their stage designer had recently added to their show for Kason's song "The Real Thing," tipped.

It came crashing down around her, the pole slamming into her ribs and knocking the wind out of her.

Kyra's mouth opened on a silent scream.

"Oh no. No. NO. NO. NO! NOOOOOO!" The fanatic stared at her, horrified, though he didn't attempt to help her get free. "I never meant for this to happen."

He began to shake as he looked from her to the sparks that began shooting from the smashed bulbs.

Oh, shit!

The spritz of sparks turned into a something steadier. A flicker, and then a small but legit fire. Kyra tried to point toward the extinguisher near her drum kit, but Number One was far too gone for that. A dark stain spread across the front of his dirty jeans then down his legs.

Kyra struggled to breathe and to move, attempting to lift the lights off her, but they were far too heavy. She was stuck. Trapped. And the flames were growing higher by the second. How the hell did the stage ignite so fast?

She remembered Ollie's recounting of the Christmas tree and thought she'd underestimated how terrified he'd been and how quickly things had gotten out of control.

"Help me," she wheezed to Number One, whose misplaced adoration had caused all this. It was a shit show when he was her best option for salvation.

It also, in some surreal way, made her realize that just

233

because she loved Ollie and Van—and she *did* love them —that if she wasn't careful, she could destroy the two men who had become everything to her. That wasn't her plan. So she had to fight.

Kyra thrashed and heaved, making the world around her dim on the edges. Except for the blaze beginning to climb higher, up the curtains on either side of the stage.

Number One looked at her with pure panic making his eyes even less sane than they'd been before. "I can't go to jail. I won't be able to go to your concerts if I'm locked up. I didn't mean to hurt you. I just...I just wanted to tell you that I'm...your Number One fan."

"You are. Thank you. Now go. Run. Get out of here." Kyra figured there was no reason for them both to die.

Number One nodded, then he bolted.

And sooner or later he was going to crash through one of Van's security barriers, which would alert security to the problem. If they didn't know by then because...

Yep. Kyra's eardrums nearly split open when fire alarms began to go off all around her. And then chaos erupted.

Someone pounded on the metal door to the wings behind her. The one she'd jammed so perfectly that even Van wouldn't be able to budge it. *Way to pick now to excel at this shit, Kyra.*

Worse, they eventually stopped.

She followed the banging as it moved around the arena floor.

Oh God. Had Number One had the same idea? Had he locked them in together? The door he'd fled through was on the opposite side of the arena. By the time someone found it, or kicked down one of the other metal doors...

It was going to be too late.

A wall of fire had formed on the edge of the stage, cutting her off from Number One's escape route.

Kyra strained and cursed. She shoved and writhed with the very real possibility of death motivating her. And yet, she barely budged the equipment, making it harder and harder to catch her breath.

Or was that the smoke, thick and dark, beginning to fill the room?

Kyra screamed and screamed but no one heard, because she'd sent them all away.

Now she was going to pay. Not only with her happiness, but with her life.

You fool!

22

Ollie had only gotten a mile or two away from the arena before he realized he couldn't do it. No matter how pitiful or likely to end up crushed it made him, he simply refused to go. Because doing so would destroy him just as surely.

After a few minutes sitting on the side of the road, he calmed down enough to actually think things through. He needed to find Van and figure out what they were going to do. If there wasn't something real between them, something more than the physical, it wouldn't work long term because Ollie knew for sure he already had feelings for Van that were growing stronger by the day. If that was the case, one of them would have to step down so Kyra at least could have a lasting relationship with the other.

If they both truly loved her, then that's all that should matter to them.

Ollie glanced over at Mr. Prickles in his cage. "I have to turn around, right?"

The hedgehog bounced up and down in the closest signal to a yes he could have made.

That cinched it.

Ollie would find Van, man up, tell him how he felt and then see where that left them.

He glanced in the rearview mirror, hoping to catch a glimpse of Kyra's gorgeous face on the electronic billboard outside of the arena as he waited for traffic to clear so he could merge into it and find somewhere to turn around. Instead, what he saw zapped his heart with terror. Horror unsurpassed even by the thought of his imploding love life and losing Kyra to another man.

Inky black smoke rose from the arena. At first it was a trickle so faint he thought his subconscious was conjuring it. But as he stared, unable to so much as blink, it grew and thickened like an evil black rope about to choke the life out of the people he loved most.

Why hadn't he heard any sirens? Why weren't fire trucks blazing down the street toward the venue? What the fuck was happening?

Ollie picked up his cell. First he texted Van. *FIRE! Get everyone out. Now!*

Then he dialed 911. He put his phone on speaker, tossed it onto the dash, then grabbed the steering wheel in hands that shook even worse than before. "Hold on, Mr. Prickles!"

He whipped the campervan around in a very illegal U-turn that nearly got him broadsided. Horns blared as vehicles swerved around him. Miraculously unscathed, he floored the campervan toward the arena. It was the longest drive of his life.

By the time he sped into the lot he'd recently left, practically on two wheels, smoke poured from the center of the arena. It was bad. Real bad.

Ollie flung open his door and dropped to the ground,

pausing only to grip the door handle until the world stopped spinning and he could draw a full breath into his chest. The acrid air stung his lungs from the inside out as it damaged his tissue.

He'd never forget that feeling as long as he lived.

"No. No. Why this? Why now? No!" Ollie shoved the specter of his mami from his memory and focused on things he might still be able to change.

He couldn't live with more ghosts haunting him.

Ollie sprinted toward the building as first a smattering, and then a deluge, of people nearly mowed him down, fleeing in the opposite direction.

Someone snagged his arm. "Buddy, you can't go in there. The whole place is going up. The sprinkler system is malfunctioning and no one can figure out why. They're evacuating the entire place."

"Where is the band?" he asked. "Are they already out?"

"I don't know. I'm just a sound tech. I think they were in their dressing rooms or something. I heard there was a big fight. They sent the rest of us away." He shook his head. "The fire started on the stage. Hopefully they saw and left."

"You mean they were closest to it." Ollie shook free and started running again. Because he knew Van and the rest of the guys. They weren't going to simply walk away from an emergency. They were going to try to be fucking heroes against a monster they couldn't fight. Well, they could fight, but they couldn't win.

And all his friends, Van and Kyra included, were right at the heart of it.

Ollie gripped the backstage door, closed his eyes, and stomped on the panic attack bubbling up within him. He was going to run in, grab them, and get the fuck out.

That's all. It was a big building. It would probably be fine.

He took his shirt off and tied it around the lower half of his face.

Then he plunged into his own personal hell, complete with heat and roaring flames.

Instantly, his eyes began to water. He felt like a salmon fighting his way upstream against the people gushing from the arena now. Even scarier was when he pushed past them all and was the only one left. It took him a minute or two longer than he hoped to find the stage in the growing confusion, and when he did, the door to it wouldn't budge.

He kicked, he threw his shoulder into it so hard he nearly dislocated it, and then he gave up. Searching for another way in, he slammed into a wall of flesh.

"Ollie? What the fuck are you doing in here?"

Van! Shit! "You have to get out of here. Where's Kyra?"

He'd never seen Van look petrified before. Not like this. His expression was nothing like the controlled irritation and purposeful manhunt he'd undertaken when Ollie had told him about Number One stalking Kyra.

This was something wild and terrible. Absolute terror.

"I think she's in there." He coughed, doubling over to try to breathe. "I've tried all the doors. They're fucked. Our only chance is going to be from outside. I have an idea."

Van grabbed Ollie's wrist and hauled him from the building despite Ollie's desire to turn around and go back in the most direct route between them and the woman they loved. "I trust you, Van. What are you thinking?"

With a curt nod of appreciation, Van crashed through a side door Ollie hadn't even noticed before and out onto some sort of loading dock. About four feet off the ground, there was a HVAC vent. Van had already busted the grate off it. The chute ran straight down to the stage where another grate was letting smoke float upward into the afternoon air.

"I can't fit in the damn thing." Van looked to Ollie. "But I think you can."

Ollie didn't hesitate. "Boost me up there."

"Go feet first so you can kick the cover off at the other end." As he gave Ollie instructions, he looped and knotted the end of a nylon tie down around Ollie's waist. "This way, I can pull you back up if you can't get through. Or if you do and the smoke is too thick or your eyes start to water too much, just tug three times and I'll yank your ass back out here. I swear, Ollie. You're going to be okay. I'm not going to let you burn like your mami."

"All I care about is Kyra." Ollie couldn't bear the thought of her in there with that malevolent smoke for another moment. "Do it. Now."

Van cupped his hands on his knee. Ollie put his sneaker in them and marveled at Van's strength. He seemed like he could have shot Ollie to the moon if he'd wanted to.

Ollie easily made it to the vent and put his legs inside. He'd never been so grateful for his less-than-broad shoulders in his entire life as he was when he rocketed down the metal chute like it was a slide. He braced himself but the two measly screws in the grate at the bottom were no impediment.

He shot out onto the stage, blinking as he tried to catch his bearings.

It was like he'd been delivered straight into the underworld.

The arena was an inferno. Timbers popped and

crackled all around him. The overwhelming panic those noises instilled in him made it even harder to breathe than the smoke. He crawled toward the back of the stage where Kyra's drum kit would be. And only when he was within ten feet of it did he hear it...coughing.

"Kyra!"

"Ollie?" More coughing. "I love you."

He didn't waste precious lungpower responding. Instead he swiped his hands out in front of him until he connected with something hard. A light stand.

And then he realized things were worse than he'd imagined. Because Kyra was trapped under the heavy equipment. He couldn't leave her there and neither could he stand to stay and watch her roast. So he grabbed the bar and lifted with every bit of strength he had.

Nothing happened.

"Kyra! You have to push. Please, try."

She blinked up at him and said, "I love you."

Clearly about to check out from smoke inhalation, she seemed dazed and unsure if he was real. He hoped he wasn't already too late. "Kyra, Van says you have to push these lights off of you to stay safe for him. Okay?"

"Van? I love him."

"I know. Me too." Ollie smiled down at her and said, "So that's why we're going to shove as hard as we can. Ready? One...two...three! PUSH!"

Together, they could move mountains. Or at least some lights.

Not very far, but enough that Kyra slipped out from beneath them. Thank God!

Ollie scooped her into his arms and tried to dash across the stage toward the faint light of the open vent, down low to the floor. It was getting so hot and so hard to breathe that he stumbled, dropping to his knees, spilling Kyra onto the floor.

It terrified him when she didn't cry out.

"Kyra! Are you okay?"

Nothing.

He grabbed her arm and dragged her to the vent. He was losing strength and consciousness. She sure as shit couldn't crawl out of the chute in her current state. He didn't have enough oxygen left to push her in front of him and Van couldn't fit. So before he could think better of it, he unwound the strap from his waist, and tied it as tightly as he could around her instead.

"I love you too, Kyra." He kissed her forehead.

Ollie fingered the leather cord lying on his chest. He lifted it from his neck and placed it over Kyra's head. If nothing else, she'd have that one picture of him and his mami to remember him by. And hopefully she'd realize that this was how things had always been meant to be.

He'd escaped once, but he wouldn't be so lucky again.

This time the right person was going to live.

For the first time, he understood how his mami had felt when she'd made this same choice. And he was proud to deserve what she'd done for him, because it had brought him here where he could pay it forward. *This* was his purpose.

With the last shred of his strength and clean oxygen, Ollie placed Kyra in the mouth of the vent, then banged three times on the side of it before he collapsed.

"Ollie! Is that you? It's getting too dangerous. I'm hauling you out," Van bellowed from the other side of the wall.

Thank God. Ollie watched as Kyra's limp form rose up toward the light. Van's strong arms would be there to catch her. He smiled as he curled into a ball and waited for darkness to descend.

The firefighters who'd caught him that night so long ago had promised his mother hadn't suffered, that the smoke had likely gotten her before the heat or flames. And that it wasn't a terrible way to go.

They had lied a little. His chest felt like it was full of razor blades.

But not for long, because he quickly became unaware of his suffering when he passed out.

23

Van was surprised at how light Ollie felt as he yanked him out of the burning building. It must be adrenaline skewing his perception. Or at least that's what he thought before he pulled another arm-length of nylon and Kyra's head poked through the wall.

"Oh, thank God!" Van's knees went weak as he reached up and took her out and down.

A crew of firefighters stormed the loading dock, screaming at him. "You can't be in here! We're taking you out, right now!"

One of them put Kyra over his shoulder and toted her away toward the fresh air and flashing lights Van now noticed behind them. As she bounced, she groaned, making Van nearly collapse with relief. She was alive at least.

"No!" He fought the first responder who tried to pry him away too. "There's someone else down there."

He jerked his thumb toward the vent, then screamed, "Ollie! I'm sending the strap back!"

Van threw it into the vent and heard it slither down, but no response came and there was no pressure on the line. So he shouted again. "Ollie!"

Nothing.

"Time to go! Leave this to us!" the fireman yelled at Van.

"Not going to happen." Van lunged for the guy and yanked the axe out of his hands.

"You're going to get yourself killed!" the man roared, but no one was crazy enough to stop an axe-wielding psychopath the size of a refrigerator, so Van made it back inside to the jammed stage door and began to hack away at it.

The firefighters quit wasting time trying to convince him to leave and instead assisted him. Three of them together were able to smash the door to smithereens then bust the rest of it down.

Van held his hand out and blindly sought the wall with the vent. It couldn't be more than twenty feet away, but it felt like twenty miles in those conditions.

When he reached the form crumpled on the floor, he thought he might be too late. Flames were licking so close to them he could no longer hear the firemen shouting at him to flee.

He didn't need to be told again.

Van lifted Ollie over his shoulder, then turned and crouched. He kept as low as possible as he ran from the stage and out his sneaky side entrance. He headed for the ambulances lining the back lot, in the direction they'd taken Kyra.

By the time he reached them, he was staggering and gasping.

Paramedics took Ollie from him, strapped an oxygen mask over his face, then started administering first aid. Van gulped down fresh air until the fringes of his vision returned to normal and he thought he could ask a question without succumbing to unconsciousness himself.

"Kyra?"

"The blonde with tattoos?" one of the emergency crew asked.

He nodded.

"She's going to be okay. Coming around now. Needs to go to the hospital. Looks like she sustained some injuries in addition to the smoke inhalation."

"Ollie?" Van croaked.

The paramedic wasn't as quick to answer this time. His lips were pressed together in a grim slash.

"Ollie?" Van insisted.

"They're doing their best to keep him here." The guy put his hand on Van's shoulder when he lurched to his feet. "Sit down. Let them work."

Yeah, not happening.

Van rushed to spot they'd taken his precious cargo and leaned over the gurney. He grabbed Ollie's hand in his and squeezed it tight. Van said then what he should have said before. "Don't go, Ollie. Please, don't go."

Still, he lay limp while the paramedics worked frantically over him.

Van leaned in and murmured, "I love you, Ollie. Kyra does too. We need you. Please don't leave us."

After a few heartbeats, Van began to lose hope.

And that's when Ollie arched off the table, his eyes flew open, and he began to hack up a lung.

Though he'd spent so much of his life surrounded by music, Van had never thought anything had sounded so beautiful before.

24

A week later, Van was thrilled to be collecting both Ollie and Kyra from the hospital. Ollie had taken a few trips through the hyperbaric oxygen chamber and they'd held Kyra because she kept Ollie calm and it tricked her into staying mostly still so her ribs had a chance to start healing.

Van hadn't left their sides in that entire time.

Still, they hadn't talked about what they would do after they'd recovered.

Now, as he rolled Kyra toward Ollie's waiting campervan while she bitched non-stop about the wheelchair they'd forced her to use, Van wasn't sure where they were headed next.

Well, okay, that wasn't exactly true. He was driving the campervan to Hot Rides, where Ollie and Kyra were going to be babied by Quinn, Trevon, Devra, Wren, Jordan, Kason, Ms. Brown, Tom, and all the Hot Rods, he was sure.

They were going to be so well cared for they wouldn't even notice if he disappeared, which he was thinking he might have to do. He'd failed. Both of his lovers had nearly died on his watch.

Kyra had been right not to trust him.

Van helped her into the campervan, where she gingerly took the bench seat next to Mr. Prickles. "Hey, little buddy. I missed you."

The hedgehog head-butted her finger through the cage.

"Aw, he missed you too," Ollie said with a laugh that morphed into another cough, followed by a groan. It was going to take a while for their bodies to recover. Van thought that was a hell of a lot faster than it would take for him to forget the things he'd seen and heard the day of the fire.

"You guys ready? I'll drive really slow and carefully, I promise. We can stop whenever you need a break." Van shut the door, then went around to the driver's side, stifling a cough of his own.

When he glanced in the mirror, he saw both Ollie and Kyra staring at him. "What? Did I forget something?"

"When are you going to stop acting like this?" Kyra asked him point blank.

"Like what?" He spun the seat around so he could face her and Ollie.

He'd been waiting for this moment. The one when they called him out and told him they were glad things hadn't worked out since he clearly wasn't the man he'd led them to believe.

"Like you're responsible for what happened to us and the pain we're in." Ollie finished Kyra's thought and she nodded in agreement.

"I *am* responsible. It was literally my job to keep Kyra safe. I couldn't. And you nearly died doing it for me." Van felt his control slipping. The past week had been torture, watching the two people he loved most suffer because of his shortcomings.

"Shut the hell up." Kyra rolled her eyes at him. "It's your job to love us."

"I do." He looked her straight in the eyes, and then Ollie too. "I love you both."

"And we love you, even when you're being stupid." She softened the sting of her barb with a dazzling smile.

"You can't always keep bad things from happening to the people you love." Ollie winced as he looked at Kyra. "That's why loving someone takes courage. I'm willing to take that chance if you are."

Kyra reached out and took one of Ollie's hands in hers before extending the other to Van.

He couldn't reject her. Never would again.

The fire had showed him how quickly everything could change. There was no time to waste in life.

So he intertwined their fingers. "I'm sorry I let you down."

"I'm sorry I didn't trust you to react reasonably to that text message." Kyra cleared her throat, then said, "If you want to blame someone for all this, it should be me."

"In your defense," Ollie joked. "He's kind of proving you were right to be worried. He didn't take it well. And it did freak me out."

Van barked out a laugh. "You're such an asshole. But you know what...I love you anyway."

"Same," Ollie said with a grin. "That's why next time, we'll all do better."

Kyra and Van repeated the words to each other and Ollie until all of them were bound together.

"Can I ask one other thing I've been wondering

about?" Kyra nibbled her lip, afraid to undo their progress but trusting that the sensitive subject couldn't break them. Only she could do that.

"Of course." Van nodded.

"What happened to Number One? Is he still...out here?" She reached over to Van and held his hand. "I'm willing to tell you, I'm afraid of running into him again. I hope you'll stick very close to me."

"You don't have to worry about that." Van stroked her hair. "Jordan apprehended him fleeing the stadium and called the authorities. He was taken to a psychiatric hospital where his mother took custody and is making sure he gets the help he needs. He won't bother you again. But if he or anyone else does, I'll be here."

"Thank you." She blew him a kiss, unshed tears making her eyes sparkle in the afternoon sun. "That makes me feel so much better."

Van relaxed as he saw she did too. She meant it. She had faith in him.

Ollie closed his eyes, leaned his head back against the headrest and said, "Hey, Van, take us home, would you?"

Van smiled as he swiveled the seat around, turned the key in the ignition, and headed for Hot Rides with his precious cargo.

25

W alker turned to Dane, who was always by his side, and said, "I swear, I can't remember a better party than this."

"We must be getting old." Dane shook his head. "Because I agree with you and there aren't any strippers or a single bottle of booze in sight. What the hell kind of New Year's Eve is this anyway?"

"A fun one. Filled with friends and family and things more important than getting off a couple times in as kinky a way as possible." Walker sighed. "Maybe we need to try something different this year."

"Like what?"

"How about a serious relationship?" he proposed as he tracked Kyra, Ollie, and Van's progress across the dance floor they'd fashioned in the center of the Hot Rides garage for the occasion.

"You mean, each of us with a woman by ourselves or one where we share someone together but for more than a night? Something like what they all have." Dane scratched the scruff on his cheek.

"Either, I guess." Walker shrugged as if it wasn't a big deal. "But if I have a choice...I vote for together."

"You have someone in mind?" Figured Dane would be able to sense the direction of his thoughts. They'd been a team for so long now. First in the service, then in a less-than-reputable biker club they'd gotten tangled up in, and finally here at Hot Rides, where they were trying to start over and make an honest living out of the thing they loved most.

Working on motorcycles.

Fortunately, Eli's father—Tom—strode in from the office, where he'd gone to answer the door. With a grim expression, he cut the music right then, saving Walker from responding. Tom slapped his palm on the garage door button. As it rose, bit by bit, a very shapely, very familiar pair of legs came into view, followed by the very person he'd been thinking of moments earlier.

What. The. Fuck.

"Hey, Walker. Is that Joy?" Dane was already climbing to his feet.

Walker would know that auburn hair and no-longer innocent, still-nervous smile anywhere. His cock never got this hard this fast for anyone else. It was her all right. Except... "Why the hell is she carrying a baby?"

"Oh, shit." Dane's eyes nearly bugged out of his head as he looked over his shoulder at Walker before rushing to take Joy and—if Walker's mental math was correct—a child that belonged to one of them in out of the cold.

They'd played by their rules. They'd only spent one night with her before moving on, but apparently it would change his life in more ways than it already had, ruining him for other flings.

Now not only would Walker never forget her, but he or Dane would be linked to her forever.

He only hoped their friendship could survive it considering they had both been in love with her for years despite the fact that her father wanted to kill them.

Walker muttered a toast to himself. "Here's to new beginnings."

He should have been more careful what he wished for.

––––

WHO'S Joy's baby's daddy and what do they plan to do about it (besides having angsty, steamy sex)? To find out, read Joy Ride by clicking HERE.

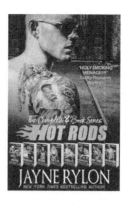

If you missed out on the Powertools: Hot Rods series, you can buy all eight books in a discounted single-volume boxset by clicking HERE.

If you'd like to start at the very beginning with the Powertools Crew, you can download a discounted boxset of the first six books HERE. Yes, know it says complete series but I wrote a seventh book more recently and haven't gotten around to updating the boxset yet, sorry! You can find the seventh Powertools book, More the Merrier, HERE.

CLAIM A $5 GIFT CERTIFICATE

Jayne is so sure you will love her books, she'd like you to try any one of your choosing for free. Claim your $5 gift certificate by signing up for her newsletter. You'll also learn about freebies, new releases, extras, appearances, and more!

www.jaynerylon.com/newsletter

WHAT WAS YOUR FAVORITE PART?

Did you enjoy this book? If so, please leave a review and tell your friends about it. Word of mouth and online reviews are immensely helpful and greatly appreciated.

JAYNE'S SHOP

Check out Jayne's online shop for autographed print books, direct download ebooks, reading-themed apparel up to size 5XL, mugs, tote bags, notebooks, Mr. Rylon's wood (you'll have to see it for yourself!) and more.
www.jaynerylon.com/shop

LISTEN UP!

The majority of Jayne's books are also available in audio format on Audible, Amazon and iTunes.

ABOUT THE AUTHOR

 Jayne Rylon is a *New York Times* and *USA Today* bestselling author who has sold more than one million books. She has received numerous industry awards including the Romantic Times Reviewers' Choice Award for Best Indie Erotic Romance and the Swirl Award, which recognizes excellence in diverse romance. She is an Honor Roll member of the Romance Writers of America. Her stories used to begin as daydreams in seemingly endless business meetings, but now she is a full time author, who employs the skills she learned from her straight-laced corporate existence in the business of writing. She lives in Ohio with her husband, the infamous Mr. Rylon, and their cat, Frodo. When she can escape her purple office, she loves to travel the world, avoid speeding tickets in her beloved Sky, SCUBA dive, hunt Pokemon, and–of course–read.

Jayne Loves To Hear From Readers
www.jaynerylon.com
contact@jaynerylon.com
PO Box 10, Pickerington, OH 43147

facebook.com/jaynerylon

twitter.com/JayneRylon

instagram.com/jaynerylon

youtube.com/jaynerylonbooks

bookbub.com/profile/jayne-rylon

amazon.com/author/jaynerylon

ALSO BY JAYNE RYLON

4-EVER

A New Adult Reverse Harem Series

4-Ever Theirs

4-Ever Mine

EVER AFTER DUET

Reverse Harem Featuring Characters From The 4-Ever Series

Fourplay

Fourkeeps

POWERTOOLS: THE ORIGINAL CREW

Five Guys Who Get It On With Each Other & One Girl. Enough Said?

Kate's Crew

Morgan's Surprise

Kayla's Gift

Devon's Pair

Nailed to the Wall

Hammer it Home

More the Merrier *NEW*

POWERTOOLS: HOT RODS

Powertools Spin Off. Keep up with the Crew plus...

Seven Guys & One Girl. Enough Said?

King Cobra

Mustang Sally

Super Nova

Rebel on the Run

Swinger Style

Barracuda's Heart

Touch of Amber

Long Time Coming

POWERTOOLS: HOT RIDES

Powertools and Hot Rods Spin Off.

Menage and Motorcycles

Wild Ride

Slow Ride

Hard Ride

Joy Ride

Rough Ride

MEN IN BLUE

Hot Cops Save Women In Danger

Night is Darkest

Razor's Edge

Mistress's Master

Spread Your Wings

Wounded Hearts

Bound For You

DIVEMASTERS

Sexy SCUBA Instructors By Day, Doms On A Mega-Yacht By Night

Going Down

Going Deep

Going Hard

STANDALONE

Menage

Middleman

Nice & Naughty

Contemporary

Where There's Smoke

Report For Booty

COMPASS BROTHERS

Modern Western Family Drama Plus Lots Of Steamy Sex

Northern Exposure

Southern Comfort

Eastern Ambitions

Western Ties

COMPASS GIRLS

*Daughters Of The Compass Brothers Drive Their Dads Crazy And
Fall In Love*

Winter's Thaw

Hope Springs

Summer Fling

Falling Softly

COMPASS BOYS

Sons Of The Compass Brothers Fall In Love

PARANORMALS

Vampires, Witches, And A Man Trapped In A Painting

Paranormal Double Pack Boxset

Picture Perfect

Reborn

PENTHOUSE PLEASURES

Naughty Manhattanite Neighbors Find Kinky Love

Taboo

Kinky

Sinner

Mentor

ROAMING WITH THE RYLONS

Non-fiction Travelogues about Jayne & Mr. Rylon's Adventures

Australia and New Zealand

Made in the USA
Coppell, TX
09 January 2021

47824466R00157